MURDER ON THE LOVERS' BRIDGE

BY

ELLEN GODFREY

CB

CONTEMPORARY BOOKS

a division of NTC/CONTEMPORARY PUBLISHING GROUP
Lincolnwood, Illinois USA

Thumbprint
Mysteries

by Ellen Godfrey.

Murder on the Loose
Murder in the Shadows

Acknowledgments

The author wishes to thank the astute and exacting
readers who helped make this novel better: Simon
Ainsworth, Mike Brodsky, Henrietta Charlie, Carmen
Johnston, Denis Johnstone, Phil Mann, Victoria
Mattsen, and Jane Stanley. Special appreciation to
Debbie Booth-Johnson and Helen Thomas of the
Victoria R.E.A.D. Society.

This is a work of fiction. The characters, incidents, and
dialogues are products of the author's imagination and are not
to be construed as real. Any resemblance to actual events or
persons, living or dead, is entirely coincidental.

Cover Illustration: David Lantz

ISBN: 0-8092-0685-4

Published by Contemporary Books,
a division of NTC/Contemporary Publishing Group, Inc.,
4255 West Touhy Avenue,
Lincolnwood (Chicago), Illinois 60646-1975 U.S.A.
© 1998 Ellen Godfrey

8 9 0 QB 0 9 8 7 6 5 4 3 2 1

CHAPTER 1

Have you ever felt that you were finally getting your act together, and then—boom!—everything falls apart? That's what happened to me.

It all began when I realized that someone was following me and I started getting these scary hang-up calls at home.

Maybe I shouldn't have been surprised. After all, in the last six months I've made a lot of enemies.

Then something really bad happened. I made a serious mistake and as a result, my friend, Nita Montez, was murdered.

Everyone tells me it wasn't my fault, but I don't agree. I'll tell you what happened, and you can decide for yourself.

I'd better tell you about Nita. Nita Montez was the last person I would have expected to be murdered. That's because Nita was a psychic. She could read your palm and tell your future. Her horoscopes were amazing. In fact, Nita was so good she made a living being psychic. Most evenings she would put on her special outfit—long, flowing skirt, a shawl with a fringe—and then go from table to table at Paul's Steakhouse. She'd read palms or do horoscopes and get good money for it.

Nita was a kind person. She'd tell her friends their futures for free. She told me that there was big trouble ahead for me and that a dangerous man would cross my path. She was sure right about that.

So why didn't she foresee her own death? I've asked myself that over and over, and I don't have an answer. Instead, Nita came to me for help. And I failed her.

My name is Janet Barkin. I have a big secret, and hardly anybody knows it. About six months ago, I won $100,000 in the lottery. That's the good news. The bad news is, my best friend's boyfriend—a guy named Baxter—thinks half the money is his.

I kept my winning a secret. I only told my closest friends and Baxter wasn't one of them. But he guessed, or thought he guessed, and he's always after me to get "his share." And I'm always denying I won.

Anyway, I couldn't spend the money on myself because then Baxter would have been sure I won. Instead, I used my winnings to start the W.R.C. That's short for Women's Rescue Company. Me and Sally Lee, my best friend, and Porsha and Mrs. Gretzky run the W.R.C. We tell everybody the company was founded by a rich old woman named Mrs. W.R. Christian. We have a little office over on Dempster Street. Last winter we helped solve the murder of some immigrant women and got ourselves on TV. After that, everyone in the neighborhood knew about us. Some people thought we were in over our heads. Some people thought we had one lucky break, and that was it. Some people thought we were really stupid.

After all, how can a bunch of women who include one overweight high school dropout (me), one blonde bimbo (Sally), one African-American teenager (Porsha), and one old lady (Mrs. Gretzky) help anybody? Sometimes I feel that way myself. Then I remember my resolution to be a tough woman and I decide to go for it.

There's a word for that, a word listed in the seven deadly sins. It's called Pride.

Maybe it was sinful pride that made me think I could help Nita Montez. Or maybe it was because she had always been so nice to me—doing my horoscope for free when I was broke. She warned me about my ex-husband, Pat, when I felt like I might go back to him—even though I knew I shouldn't. Nita told me that Sagittarius (my sign) and Scorpio (Pat's sign) were bad news together. She said it would never work. Nita said that Scorpios like to control and Sagittarians don't like being controlled. When I felt like I couldn't make it alone, Nita told me I could. She said she saw it in the stars.

So when Nita came into the W.R.C. office that afternoon three weeks ago, right away I wanted to do what I could to help.

I remember it was a scorching hot afternoon. Outside our office on Dempster Street the cars seemed to go by in a shimmer of heat. The sky was a dull blue and from time to time there were sudden flashes of heat lightning. My daddy always called summer lightning the devil's pitchfork, and with that heat, you could imagine the devil at work. My shirt stuck to my chest, and my new short haircut had completely frizzed up. Another bad hair day.

The door opened.

Lech, my German shepherd guard dog, looked up from his place under my desk. My desk is actually more like a table, so Lech can see most of the office by sticking his head out. I'm not sure why he likes it under there. Maybe he thinks it's cooler. His tongue was hanging out and he was panting gently in the heat.

When Lech saw it was Nita at the door, he dropped his head back down on his paws. He knew he didn't have to guard me against Nita.

"Hi, Janet. Hi, Lech," Nita said. She came in and flopped down on a chair. "Boy, it's hot." Nita had thick, wavy black hair. She lifted it up off her neck to cool herself. "Hey, Janet, I like your hair. Did Sally cut it for you? In this heat, short hair is a smart move."

"Yes. But it looked better when she did it," I said. Sally works at a classy hair salon, Hair-Today. My style was supposed to be the new cool cut. It had looked good in the picture Sally showed me. It had looked good when Sally finished styling it. But that was last week. Now I looked like the before in a before-and-after ad.

I was the only one in the office that afternoon. Porsha was at school and Sally was at the salon. She only worked at the W.R.C. part-time. "So, what's up?" I asked Nita.

"Oh, Janet," Nita said.

I looked at Nita and realized she was crying. I got up and went to her. I put my arms around her and gave her a hug. "It's okay," I said. Lech got up too. He trotted over to Nita and pushed his nose gently into her knee, which was his way of comforting her.

"Can you believe it, Lech?" Nita sobbed, looking into his soft brown eyes. "I've made such a hash of things. I wish I were a dog like you. I'd hide under the desk and never come out."

"What's the problem?" I asked. I went over to my desk and got a box of Kleenex which I handed to Nita. She took a piece and wiped her face carefully, so as not to smear her mascara.

"It's Paul," Nita said. "He won't leave me alone. He's scaring me. I don't know what to do. You've got to help me."

"Of course we will," I said. "That's what we're here for." But inside I was feeling scared too. I knew about Paul Moro. He was really a nice guy most of the time. But he was a little crazy where Nita was concerned. Scary crazy.

"Janet, do you think you could talk to him? Tell him he's got to stop it. Make him stop it."

"Stop what?" I asked.

Nita said, "I told him, 'Paul, it's over. It's no good. Go back to your wife. You have kids. It was a big mistake. It's not fair to her and it's not fair to me.' But he won't accept it. He says it's written in the stars. We're meant to be lovers for eternity. Like Romeo and Juliet."

I tried to keep a straight face. After all, I saw the movie. Romeo and Juliet were teenagers. Nita is about my age. I'm twenty-four. But Paul Moro is old. I mean, he must be close to fifty! He is bald on top and has a stomach that hangs down over his belt. He does wear cool clothes, he drives a flashy car, and he owns his own restaurant, Paul's Steakhouse. He has enough energy to be a teenager. But Romeo, he isn't. And besides, as Nita says, he's married and has four kids. I'm pretty sure Romeo wasn't married and having a thing with Juliet on the side.

Nita must have seen what I was thinking. "Don't laugh, Janet. Paul is just as crazy as Romeo. And look what happened to *him*."

"He died, right?" I said.

"Right," Nita said, and I could tell she wished Paul Moro would die too. Or at least get out of her life.

"Anyway," Nita continued, "Paul follows me everywhere. He's wrecking my business. Yesterday, I was doing a reading for one of Sally's clients from Hair-Today. A really rich lady. I went to this big house in Glencoe. I had her charts all done up in this beautiful folder with a zodiac on the cover and everything. She was totally impressed. It looked so professional. Then Paul—he ruined *everything*. He was driving back and forth outside in that ugly Mustang he has with the top down. Then he started honking his horn. I pretended like I didn't hear. Then he drove up the driveway, got out, and looked right in the living room window!"

"Why did he do that?"

"Because he thought I might be with another man! I can't take it any longer, Janet. I can't." Nita grabbed a fresh Kleenex from the box just in time, because tears had begun gushing from her eyes. "He's ruining my life!"

I knew just how Nita felt. My ex, Pat, hounds me too. He says he wants me back. Even though he tells me I am stupid and fat and a loser, he still wants me back. When a man goes out of control, it can be really scary.

"Don't worry, Nita," I said. "The W.R.C. will take care of it."

Nita looked at her watch. "It's almost five. This is a busy time for him. Maybe you could go over about eleven tomorrow morning? To the restaurant? That's the best time to talk to him."

"I'll do it," I said, wondering what in the world I could say to Paul Moro to get him to back off.

Nita got up. Her eyes looked swollen and her nose was red. I walked her to the door. "By the way, Janet," Nita said.

"Yes?"

"I heard some bad news. You know Roach Roads?"

I knew Roach Roads. He was a slimy crook and a murderer, and I had been responsible for sending him to jail for murder six months ago. "Yes," I said. "How do you know him?"

"Not me. Paul. Paul used to pay him money every month before he went to jail. All the neighborhood restaurants had to. Some kind of a payoff. Anyway, he's out."

"What?!" My heart started to bang in my chest. I knew Roach Roads wanted revenge against me. He had been sentenced to twenty years with a chance of parole in ten and he blamed me. How could he be out of jail in six months? "That's impossible!" I said. My voice came out in a kind of croak.

"You'd think so," Nita said, opening the front door. A blast of heat came into the office. It felt almost like a hot, wet hand, pressing on my chest. "But he's out. Paul said he came around to the restaurant to say that he'd be collecting personally now that he's back."

"Did Roach say anything else?" I asked faintly. *Like, did he say he wanted to kill me?* I thought to myself.

"I don't know," Nita said. "You can ask Paul when you talk to him tomorrow."

"I'll do that," I said.

After Nita left, I closed up the office. I wanted to go home and get Mrs. Gretzky's advice. And I was scared too. At my desk alone in the office in front of a big plate glass window that looked over Dempster Street, I felt like a sitting duck. I was so nervous, I even thought about calling my ex-husband Pat. Pat is an undercover policeman, so he could tell me about Roach, but I knew that would be a mistake.

All the way home, walking in the stifling heat, I wanted a cigarette. Six months of not smoking, and I still wanted a cigarette. It didn't help that I had this weird feeling—like someone was watching me. A sort of prickling on the back of my neck.

I opened the front door of the old house where I live, and the hot stuffy air almost choked me. Mrs. Gretzky owns the house. She made it into three apartments. She lives in the basement, Porsha and her mama live on the ground floor, and I live on the second floor. The basement apartment is the coolest in the summer. I thought I would go down and ask Mrs. Gretzky's advice. But first I had to change my clothes. They were soaked with sweat. And I wanted to give Lech a drink. His tongue was hanging out and he was panting.

The stairwell was like an oven. I went up slowly, Lech behind me. I opened the door and the phone started to ring. I dashed over and picked it up. "Hello?" I said.

Silence.

"Hello? Anyone there?"

No answer. I thought I could hear breathing. There was something sinister and frightening about the silence and the steady breathing at the other end.

"Oh, get a life!" I said into the phone and slammed it down.

Now I was really nervous. I filled Lech's water bowl and he lapped it up in an instant, spattering water over the kitchen floor. I refilled it and he drank that down too. Then he collapsed on the floor, his tongue hanging out. I opened the kitchen window as wide as I could, but the air outside was so hot and there was no breeze, so it did little good.

I took a shower and changed my clothes. Then I phoned downstairs, checking to see if Mrs. Gretzky was home. She wasn't. I walked restlessly around my apartment. I wanted a cigarette. I wanted to call someone. But I couldn't decide what to do. Who was calling me? How could Roach Roads be out of jail so soon? Was it he who was making the hang-up calls? But they had been going on for weeks, and Roach was just out. Or was he? What could I say to Paul Moro that would help Nita?

I walked faster. I walked into the living room and turned on the TV. Then I turned it off. I needed to do something. I caught sight of a cardboard box in the corner. Some old papers I had brought with me when I left Pat and came to live on my own. I had meant to sort through it and throw out the junk, but I never seemed to get to it. I took the box into the kitchen and set it on the kitchen table.

I opened the box. On the top was a pile of photographs. I spread them out on the kitchen table. Now I remembered why I hadn't wanted to open this box.

The pictures were of me and Pat in happier times. The first one I looked at was of Pat and me at the beach. I had a towel wrapped around my hips to hide the flab, but Pat looked like a movie star. His black hair was gelled and shone in the sun, and he posed so you could see he had a perfect body. When I was in high school, all the girls were in love with Pat. I had felt so lucky when he chose me. I couldn't believe it—it felt like a dream come true. Nothing mattered to me but Pat. I used to write his name over and over on my notebook. Pat Barkin, Pat Barkin, Pat Barkin.

I picked up another picture. It was Pat with some of his friends from the police force. They were standing in front of Paul Moro's old Mustang, laughing. Pat had a beer bottle in his hand. Pat often had a beer bottle in his hand. When we were married, I remember Pat coming home late, smelling of stale beer and another woman's perfume. I remember the look on his face when I asked him where he'd been. I remember him shouting at me that it was none of my business.

Something fell on the picture. It was a tear. Pat had said he loved me, that he still loved me. But I did not know what he meant.

I gathered up the pictures. I wanted to throw them in the garbage. But I couldn't do it. I put them back in the box, put the box back in the corner, and picked up the telephone to call Mrs. Gretzky.

CHAPTER 2

I knocked and Mrs. Gretzky opened the door. "Janet! What's the matter?" Mrs. Gretzky said even before I could open my mouth.

Mrs. Gretzky is in her seventies. She has gray hair in a frizzy perm and is even fatter than me. She wears flowered housedresses like you see on old TV shows. Today her face was red, and as she stepped back to let me in, I could see that her legs were bothering her. Both her ankles were all swollen up.

"Let's go into the living room—the kitchen is too hot," Mrs. Gretzky said. "You sit down and I'll get you something cold to drink. I can tell from your face, you got troubles."

I started to tell her not to bother, but she had already headed off. Lech trotted after her. He knew his mother would be in her usual place, under the kitchen table, and he wanted to hang out with her. Mrs. Gretzky's dog,

11

Teresa, is Lech's mother. When Teresa had puppies, Mrs. Gretzky gave me the one she had named Lech Walesa. The real Lech Walesa is a famous Polish guy who is a hero of Mrs. Gretzky's.

Mrs. Gretzky came back with two glasses of iced tea. She sat me down on a chair and turned the fan so it would blow on me.

Then she collapsed onto the sofa with a big sigh. "Oof," she said. "This heat—it's killing me. Last night, I didn't sleep a wink. Your Lech is feeling it, I can see. Just now, he drank my Teresa's water. But it's okay—I gave them both some more."

Mrs. Gretzky's has a deeply lined face and wise, sad eyes that look as if they have seen a lot in a long, hard life. Looking at her, I felt bad to see how the heat was getting to her. Although only half a mile from Lake Michigan, our neighborhood doesn't get the lake breezes.

"So?" she said.

"Trouble," I said. "First, Nita Montez wants the W.R.C. to get Paul Moro to leave her alone. He's stalking her."

Mrs. Gretzky frowned. "That's bad," she said.

"And Roach Roads is out of jail," I said.

"Aach, that's *really* bad," Mrs. Gretzky said. "But you look like something else is bothering you. Am I right?"

"I got another one of those hang-up calls," I confessed.

"And?" Mrs. Gretzky said.

"And that's all," I said.

Mrs. Gretzky shook her head like she didn't believe me. "You're not missing that bum of a husband of yours, are you?" she asked.

See what I mean about her being wise? "How did you know that?" I asked her.

"I can tell by your face," Mrs. Gretzky said. "Mark my words and write it in a book, that man is no good for you."

"That's just what Nita told me," I said sadly. "And you are both right. I told him it was over and I walked out on him. What more can I do?"

Mrs. Gretzky looked unconvinced.

There was a knock on the door. "I'll get it," I said. I jumped up and went to the door. I opened it on the security chain, saw Sally, and let her in.

Sally followed me into the living room. Her face was glowing. Her blonde hair was cut in a new short punky style that made her blue eyes look bigger and shinier than ever. "Hi, Janet! Hi, Mrs. Gretzky! Where's my darling Lech?" Sally said. Without waiting for an answer, she dashed into the kitchen and I could hear her talking to Lech. "Hiya, Lech! How's my darling doggie? Mmmm, here's a kiss!" Then Sally bounced back into the living room.

"You're sure in a good mood," I said.

"Janet, oh, my God, your hair! Didn't you use that gel mist I gave you? You've got to do that first thing if you don't want it to frizz."

"Never mind my hair," I said. "What's up?"

"Baxter and I are back together!" Sally said. She danced around the room. "He said he's sorry about all the bad stuff he did and he's got a new job. He's like, totally changed!"

I felt my heart sink. I knew Sally loved Baxter, but he was really a bad guy. He had worked for Roach Roads, and he had been mixed up with the murder of the immigrant women. He had beaten Sally in the past. Could he really change that much? I didn't think so. And he was still after my lottery money.

I had trusted Sally with the secret of the lottery money because she had been my best friend forever. But love makes people do strange things and I feared Sally might betray me to Baxter.

"That's great, Sally," I said. "I'm happy for you."

"You don't sound like you think it's great," Sally said, sitting down and looking at me. "Don't worry, I won't tell him about the lottery money or that you really own the W.R.C."

"Promise?" I said.

"Of course, I promise," Sally said.

Lech came trotting into the room. He looked at me and I realized he probably wanted to go out. He had drunk his own water and Teresa's water so it wasn't surprising. Then I should take him upstairs and get him some dinner. I could use some food too.

"Look," I said to Mrs. Gretzky. "Why don't you explain the problems about Nita and Roach to Sally? I need to take Lech for a walk and while I'm out, I can pick up a pizza. It's too hot to cook. We can decide what to do about Nita when I get back."

They both agreed.

Lech and I set off. Lech doesn't need a leash because I've trained him to heel. We headed for the park across the street. Sometimes kids play there, but mostly it's people doing illegal deals of one kind or another. The grass is worn away and the ground is littered with junk, but Lech finds it interesting.

As soon as we got there, something odd happened. First I felt that weird prickling on the back of my neck again, just as I had when I was walking home from the office—like someone was watching me. As I'd done before, I looked around, but I just saw the usual sights. A few kids were lounging around. A stray dog I'd seen before was curled up in the shade of the lone tree in the middle of the park. Cars drove by. Just like always.

Then one of the kids darted toward me. I didn't know his name, but I thought I'd seen him around. "Hey, Lech!" he shouted. "I got a Big Mac for you."

This was odd. Lech is not a friendly dog unless I let him be. I had never talked to this kid. How did he know Lech? Why did he care about him? Why would a strange kid give him a treat? And how did the kid know that Lech's favorite thing in the world is Big Macs?

The kid pulled a Big Mac out of its container and threw it down in front of Lech. Then he and his friends jumped on their skateboards and took off.

Lech looked at me. He didn't touch the burger. I knew he was hungry. His mouth was open and his tongue was hanging out. He really wanted that burger. But I had trained Lech never to take food except from me or from people he knew and trusted, because that's something guard dogs need to know. So Lech was waiting for my okay.

Meanwhile, the stray dog had uncurled. He'd smelled the burger and was on his way toward us.

Lech looked at me pleadingly.

Something about the whole thing didn't feel right to me. I couldn't decide what to do. While I tried to figure it out, the other dog ran up and grabbed the burger. Now Lech gave me a humiliated, pleading look. His expression said, 'That burger is mine!' and it also said, 'I could take that stray with two paws tied behind my back!'

"No, Lech," I said. I patted him. "Good dog. Stay."

Lech remained still as a statue, watching the stray. His mouth was open and drool dripped off his tongue, but he didn't move.

The stray ran off to the other side of the tree, dropped

the burger, and gobbled it up.

Then he trotted back toward us. I think he had decided Lech was a wuss and he was going to take him out. But suddenly he staggered. His lips pulled back over his teeth as if he were grinning and his body went stiff. He collapsed and just lay there, his eyes rolled back in his head.

I stared at him. For a minute I didn't get it, then I did. I knelt down and hugged Lech as hard as I could. He licked my face. "Good dog," I said. I went over and checked the stray.

He was dead.

I needed to get out of there. I said to Lech, "Let's go. I'm going to buy you your very own Big Mac."

With Lech at my side, I set off down the street, sick at heart over that poor stray, but thankful Lech had escaped unharmed. I felt a little better as we left the little park behind, but still I had the weird feeling of someone watching me.

Half an hour later, Lech had wolfed down the Big Mac I had bought for him, and I was standing at the Pizza Palace waiting for my order.

"Janet! Hello again!"

It was Nita.

"Hi, Nita," I said.

Nita had changed into her psychic outfit. She had on a long filmy skirt and a tight black tank top with sparkly silver moons and stars on it. Her hair was piled on top of her head. She had heavy black eyeliner around her eyes and thick dark red lipstick on. I thought she looked sensational.

"It's too hot to cook," Nita said. "I thought I'd stop by and get a slice before I have to be at work."

"Don't they give you free food at Paul's restaurant?" I asked. Although Nita lived in the neighborhood, I had never seen her at the Pizza Palace before.

Nita drew herself up so that she was standing tall as a queen. "I wouldn't take a bite to eat from that man if I was starving!" she said.

"Wow," I said. "That bad, is it?"

"Do you know what he did now?" Nita demanded.

I shook my head.

"He sent me a box of flowers!"

"Excuse me, but what's so awful about a box of flowers?" I said, puzzled.

Nita leaned over and put her face close to mine. "Awful? I'll tell you what was so awful. They were dead! Stinking dead. Can you believe it? I opened the box and it was full of gross, smelly, rotting flowers." Nita's eyes got bigger. "They were roses and the petals had all gone black."

"Oh, Nita," I said.

"It was like the most evil omen. I opened that box and I saw death looking back at me!"

"What do you mean?" I asked.

Nita looked past me, as if she were looking at something in her mind. "Paul was sending me a message that I was killing our love." She pressed her fist against her heart. "He's got to stop this, Janet. Make him understand, *he* killed our love, not me."

"I'll try. But he sounds like he's kind of crazy."

Nita nodded. "I know. But you helped those other women against Roach Roads. Paul is no big criminal, so handling him's got to be easier." She put a hand to her mouth and I saw that her hand was trembling. "I can't take much more of this. It's like living in a nightmare. I try and try to wake up, but when I do, I'm still in the nightmare."

"Here's your pizza, Janet," said the kid behind the counter. He handed me the box.

"I'll talk to him tomorrow and let you know how it goes," I promised.

Nita leaned over and gave me a hug. "I'm sure you'll find a way to get him to stop," she said.

I took my pizza and left. Lech trotted along beside me. Again I felt that strange feeling, and now I saw that Lech was feeling it too. The hair around his neck was up, his tail was stiff, and he was looking around. I looked too, but there was nothing to see except the usual traffic and people.

If someone was following me, I would never be able to pick him out on a busy street.

I walked on. Then I heard the sound of running footsteps, and someone called my name.

"Hey, Janet! Baby!" It was Pat. He caught up to me. "I went by your place, and when you weren't there, I stopped by Mrs. Gretzky's. Sally told me you were at the Pizza Palace. I was hoping to get you before you got your pizza, but it looks like I was too late."

"Why?" I asked.

"Why?" Pat said. He ran his hand over his hair. Pat was looking good. He was wearing a tight T-shirt with the sleeves cut off so you could see the muscles in his arms. He was tan and his teeth looked very white when he smiled at me. "I need to talk to you. I thought we could have some dinner together. A couple of drinks. You know."

"No, I don't know," I said. I had stopped walking. Lech stood by me, watching, waiting for my command. I had got Lech after I left Pat, so Lech did not consider Pat a friend.

"What do you want to talk to me about?"

"Come on, Janet," Pat said. "Don't be that way. Hey, what did you do to your hair, for God's sake? Looks like you had a run-in with a lawn mower."

"I'm taking the pizza back to have dinner with Mrs. Gretzky and Sally," I said. "So just tell me what's on your mind. I'm in a hurry. I don't want the pizza to get cold."

Pat had been smiling at me. Now he stopped smiling. A worried look came over his face. "Janet, do you know Roach Roads is out on appeal?"

"I know he's out," I said.

"Aren't you worried? If you're not, you should be. You shouldn't be living alone, Janet. You need someone to protect you," Pat said.

"What? Are you volunteering?" I asked.

"It's my job!" Pat said. "You're my wife."

Pat and I were officially divorced, but somehow it didn't seem to have sunk in.

"Pat," I began, "I told you a hundred times—"

Pat put up his hand. "You're not listening, Janet. Read my lips: Roach Roads is out of jail. He can't operate on the street with people thinking he was taken down by some dumb chick. He has to come after you. He has to take you out. Don't you see?"

"Yes," I said. "I see. He tried it before. It didn't work then and it isn't going to work now."

"He's put it on the line," Pat said. "He's told everybody you are going down. He says he is going to do it in a slow, painful way to be sure you suffer. He wants you to pay for what you did to him. He's a real nasty guy, and he still has a lot of powerful friends. You have to take this seriously."

"I do," I said. "I got the message, thank you. Now if you will excuse me—"

"Janet," Pat said. His voice was no longer commanding. It was pleading. I had never heard Pat plead before, and I realized that he was worried about me. I was touched, but I didn't want him to know that.

I turned away from him. "Heel, Lech!" I said. And Lech and I took off down the street. After a half a block, I looked back.

Pat was still standing on the sidewalk where I had left him. His face was twisted up with rage. People moved around him, but Pat just stood there, looking after me, as if he were frozen to the spot, too angry to move.

CHAPTER 3

Paul's Steakhouse is a place where, inside, it always feels like night. The windows have a kind of yellow pebbly glass that keeps out the light, and they have candles on all the tables. They have white tablecloths, fake flowers on each table, and giant menus encased in plastic. Paul's is famous for their huge steaks. You can get a twelve-ounce porterhouse steak, baked potato, and choice of sides for $12.95. Lots of people think that is a bargain, but it is not the kind of place I go to. I tend to hang out at places where you can see what you are eating and where they don't bother with tablecloths. Cheaper places.

When I got there at eleven the morning after Nita asked for my help, the restaurant was closed. I ignored the 'Closed, Open at 11:30' sign and tried the front door. It opened and I went in. The place was deserted. The tables were all set and bright overhead lights shone down on everything. I had never seen Paul's under bright lights, and it looked different somehow. Less glamorous. You could tell that the flowers on the table and the plants in the corners were fake, and that they were dusty.

A door in the back opened and Paul bustled out. He was yelling at someone behind him as he came through the swinging door. "You don't tell *me* what to do!" Paul shouted. "I'm the boss! You do what I say or you're outta here. It's my way or the highway, get it?"

He caught sight of me and the angry look vanished from his face, to be replaced by a big smile. "Janet!" he cried. He hurried toward me and threw his arms around me. "Janet! Look at you! Gorgeous. I like that haircut! It's hot!"

I didn't know Paul that well, but it didn't matter. Paul was full of energy and enthusiasm. Everyone was either his best buddy or his worst enemy. Right now, he was treating me warmly because he knew I was Nita's friend. Paul was wearing a white shirt and black pants with pleats in the front. His shirt was partly unbuttoned and I could see several gold medals hanging on gold chains on his chest. His bald head shone in the bright lights, the black hair on the sides was slicked back, and he smelled strongly of aftershave lotion.

"We're not open yet," he said, "but for you, we're always open. What can I get you? A coffee? Early lunch? A glass of wine?"

"Paul, I came to talk to you about Nita," I said.

The smile disappeared from his face. A look of deep sadness replaced it. "She's mad at me, isn't she? I played a dirty trick on her. I know—don't tell me—it was a mistake. I wasn't thinking straight when I did it. But she'll get over it. She loves me."

I walked over to the bar and sat down on one of the stools. Paul went around behind the bar. He took down a bottle and poured himself a drink of something yellow.

He drank it down. He poured out more for himself and one for me and pushed it toward me. I took a sip. It was disgusting. Sweet and bitter at the same time.

He saw my expression. "You don't like that? It's Cynar, an Italian drink, made of artichoke leaves. Superb." He took another sip and smacked his lips. Then he frowned. "Nita didn't like it either, but I told her she must keep trying. Sooner or later she would learn to appreciate it."

"Paul, Nita wants you to leave her alone."

Paul smiled. "No, she doesn't. Not really. You don't know Nita like I do. She's a passionate woman, and she needs me to prove my love to her. She must have thought I was taking her for granted, so she is giving me a hard time. Don't worry, I'm not one of those men who give up at the first setback. I've got persistence and determination—that's how come I'm so successful. Do you think I would have all this," he spread his arms out to indicate the restaurant, "if I gave up at the first obstacle?"

"But, Paul—" I began.

"A beautiful young woman like Nita, she has to be courted, pursued, conquered!" Paul said. "I understand this. I am Italian, you know. We Italians, we are the world's greatest lovers. Did Romeo give up when Juliet's family said he couldn't have her?"

"Just a moment," I interrupted him. "It's not Nita's family we're talking about. It's Nita. She told you it's over. She meant it."

"No, no, she doesn't," Paul said. "You don't understand her the way I do."

"Listen, Paul," I said. "I'm not kidding. Nita came to me and asked the W.R.C. to help her. You are driving her crazy. She wants to lead her life and move on. You and her—it's over. Finished."

"I don't have to listen to this," Paul said. "You got some kind of problem? Is that why you're butting into my business? You think because you were on TV you know everything, is that it? Well, let me tell you something. You should be worrying about yourself, not Nita and me. Roach Roads is telling everybody you aren't long for this world, do you get my drift?"

"But don't you see? Following her everywhere, sending her things, that's not love. You're scaring her. She hates it."

"I'll stop when she comes back where she belongs," Paul said. "Until then, I have to keep an eye on her, prove to her I love her." He was not smiling now. In fact, he had the same expression he'd had when he yelled into the kitchen that he was the boss.

"If you don't leave Nita alone, the W.R.C. is going to have to take action against you," I said. I had no idea what I meant by these words; they just popped out of my mouth.

"Take action? What the hell does that mean?"

"You'll find out."

"I think you better go now. I have work to do," Paul said. Then he leaned over the bar. There was a crazy look in his eyes. "I love Nita more than life itself," he said. "And she loves me. This is a love beyond anything you can imagine. You tell me it's over between Nita and me? It will never be over. That woman is mine." He looked right at me and I felt a chill go down my spine. Then he looked away and poured himself another drink.

I got down from my bar stool and left.

*   *   *

It was noon when I got back to the W.R.C. office. We had scheduled a lunch meeting to discuss what to do if my talking to Paul didn't work.

Sally and Porsha were both there. They had brought

sandwiches. I had stopped at the doughnut shop next door and picked up a dozen of my favorites, the kind with chocolate frosting and chocolate sprinkles. Mrs. Gretzky couldn't make it; her legs weren't up for the walk. We would have to fill her in later.

As soon as everyone was settled, I told them about my conversation with Paul. "I couldn't get through to him," I confessed. "He figures Nita is his woman and he can do what he wants."

"She's not even his wife," Sally said.

"So what if she was his wife?" Porsha said. "That idea of owning a woman, that went out in the Middle Ages. Wife or not, doesn't matter. A woman as property—that's slavery, girl."

I don't know if I told you, but Porsha is a genius. She gets straight A's in school and she's reading all the time. But what's really amazing is that Porsha is street-smart too. She used to be kind of funny-looking, but now that she's sixteen, she's starting to get pretty. The rest of her is catching up to her long, skinny legs. She wears her hair in a mass of tiny braids, threaded through with colored beads. She has a collection of glasses with big frames in different colors. Her skin is the color of a shiny new penny, and she has sparkling brown eyes.

"He thinks he has a right to follow her and harass her," I said. "He thinks it's okay. He has no idea how terrified she is. Or if he does, he doesn't care."

"I wonder how he'd feel if some girl was following him everywhere and hassling him when he was trying to work," Porsha said. "Bet he'd sing a different tune then."

"That's it!" I said.

"What?" Sally asked.

"Let's give him a taste of his own medicine. Let's stalk

him. See how he likes it. Let's send him disgusting presents and give him hang-up calls at home. We could even put up posters about him around the neighborhood that say, 'Watch out for the stalker.'"

"Wait a minute," Sally said. "He has a wife. She didn't do anything. She shouldn't be punished or embarrassed."

"Okay," I said. "We won't bother him at home. But at the restaurant, on the street, everywhere, we'll let him see what it feels like to be terrorized by crazy people stalking you."

"I don't know . . ." Sally said. "I have a bad feeling about that idea."

I was surprised. Ever since we all started the W.R.C. together, we've worked as a team. We get our ideas together, and we've never disagreed. "Porsha? What do you think?" I asked.

"I love it, man," Porsha said. "We'll show that Romeo not to mess with the Capulets."

"Capulets?" Sally said. "Has Paul been sending Nita some kind of pills?"

"No," Porsha said. "Capulet is the last name of Juliet's family in the Romeo and Juliet story. They were the ones who wanted revenge on Romeo when he wouldn't lay off of Juliet. That's in Shakespeare's play. I meant, we're like the Capulets, you know? We're protecting Nita like they protected Juliet in the story."

"Oh," said Sally, looking confused. "I thought Juliet died because of her family being against Romeo. She did in the movie."

I didn't like the direction this conversation was taking. "When we talked about this last night over pizza, we didn't have any ideas," I said. "This is the best one we've come up with. I'm going to call Mrs. Gretzky, see what she says."

I called Mrs. Gretzky and explained our plan. I was sure she would get behind my idea. Mrs. Gretzky was a fighter. But she surprised me. "No, no," she said. "That's not good. You give him a dose of his own medicine, you think that will change his mind?"

"Yes," I said. "He doesn't understand. He thinks Nita is powerless. He thinks he can do what he wants, and when she realizes he won't change, she'll come back to him. We want him to know what it feels like to be stalked and followed."

Mrs. Gretzky was silent for a moment. Then she said, "It sounds good when you say it like that. But when a man is in love, he doesn't think straight."

I turned to Porsha and Sally. "Mrs. Gretzky thinks it won't work. She says when a man's in love, he doesn't think straight." I held the phone out to them.

"That's not love, what Paul's doing," Porsha said loudly, so Mrs. Gretzky could hear. "That's a power trip."

I talked to Mrs. Gretzky some more. In the end, she wasn't happy, but she agreed. Sally went along too. I could see she thought it would be fun to stalk Paul Moro, but she still had her bad feeling. Porsha and I, on the other hand, were 100 percent behind the idea. So we divided most of the work up between us. Porsha agreed to get some of her teenage friends to help. She also typed up some letters on the computer. The first one went like this:

August 4, 1998

Dear Paul:

We are watching you. Wherever you go, we will be there. Whatever you do, we will see you. When you awake in the morning, our eyes will be upon you. When you drift away to sleep, we will be watching. You can have no secrets from us.

Even in your most secret dreams, there we will be. Many of the people you see on the street are secretly our eyes and ears. They report to us. What you do shall be known to us in every detail. We are following, watching, waiting.

Paul, we will give you no peace until you abandon your pursuit of Nita Montez. You do not own Nita. Nita does not belong to you. She is her own woman. If she says she wishes to be free of you, you must accept it.

Until you do, we will give you no peace. Night and day, our eyes are upon you.

Beware!

Sincerely,

Friends of Nita Montez

Isn't that great? Didn't I tell you Porsha was a genius? The other letters were just as good. They all ended with the word *beware*. Porsha made the computer print *beware* in scary type, so it looked like the ad for a horror movie. I would hate to get a letter like that and I felt sure Paul would think twice once *he* got it. I should have stopped and asked myself *what* he would think twice, but I guess the sin of Pride blinded me to what was about to happen.

*   *   *

I couldn't take the first shift of following and hassling Paul Moro because I had a date that night. Well, maybe I exaggerate when I call it a date. I hoped it was a date, but maybe Larry Keegan thought of it as a chance to catch up with an old friend.

Larry Keegan was a lieutenant at the local precinct. When the W.R.C. solved the case of the immigrant women, I had hoped my ex-husband Pat—who is also a cop—would help. He couldn't, so we turned to Larry. Not long after Roach Roads was convicted, Larry was sent away on a training course. A couple of weeks ago, I heard he was back in town and I found myself looking for him everywhere. Then he called me and suggested we get together to "catch up." I was supposed to meet him at Sai Woo's, a local Chinese restaurant.

I was late. I had changed my clothes three times. I had put so much spray gel on my hair that it got hard as a helmet—a frizzy helmet—so I had to wash it and dry it and start all over. Finally I gave up the losing battle of trying to look glamorous and took off for Sai Woo's.

As soon as I walked into the restaurant, I saw Larry. He was sitting at a far table, and even across the room, I could see his clear blue eyes. They gave me a quivery feeling, as if he could look inside of me and see how much I liked him. Larry was a tall, thin guy who had a kind smile. I trusted Larry, but I was not sure I should. After all, I had trusted Pat, and look where that got me.

Larry stood up politely when I came near. It made me feel strange. But I managed to smile and act normal, and soon we were chatting away as if he had never left town. He told me he liked my hair, and I pretended to believe him. I asked him about the course he had been on and he explained, and that lasted us until the fortune cookies.

Then Larry said, "Janet, there's some stuff we need to talk about."

Here it comes, I thought. He's going to warn me about Roach Roads.

Sure enough, Larry said, "You know Roach Roads is out on appeal?"

"Everyone is telling me. Everyone's warning me. But what am I supposed to do?" I said, starting to get worked up. "Run away and hide or something?"

"No, of course not," Larry said. "I know how important the W.R.C. is to you. And you guys are doing good work.

You can't let Roach scare you away."

"Right!" I said. I couldn't believe it. Larry Keegan was on our side. "That's what I think he's trying to do," I said, "scare us. After all, Roach doesn't dare go after me. If anything happened to me, he'd be the first suspect. And anyway, I have Lech to protect me."

"Where is Lech?" Larry asked.

"Outside. I take him with me everywhere. He's trained to wait if I tell him to."

"I think you're right about what Roach is doing," Larry said. "I think he's trying to scare you. The word on the street is that he intends to have you snatched and then torture you. Everybody's heard the story. But you have to ask yourself, how come everybody knows? That never used to be Roach's way. He never talked about what he planned to do. He just did it."

I thought that maybe getting arrested, tried, convicted, and sent to jail might have changed the way Roach did business, but I didn't say it.

"Hey, Janet!" said a voice behind me.

I turned around. It was Pat. "Hello, Pat," I said. "What are you doing here?"

"I saw Lech outside and I figured you were inside having dinner." Pat looked at Larry. I realized Pat was really angry. He had that just-about-to-boil-over look that I remembered from when we were married. I knew something bad was about to happen.

"Keegan, I want to talk to my wife. Take a hike," Pat said to Larry.

Larry looked at me.

"Larry and I are having dinner together, Pat," I said. "And I am not your wife."

"You heard her," Larry said. "If you need to talk to Janet, do it some other time."

Pat grabbed at my shoulder. "Let's go," he said.

"Don't touch me!" I shouted. I jerked away from his fingers.

Larry stood up. "You're out of line," he said to Pat. His voice was very calm. "Can't you see she doesn't want to talk to you?"

Pat's skin went white around his lips, and his hands clenched into fists. For a moment I thought he was going to throw a punch. But he got himself under control. He looked at me, and I saw something in his eyes that made me feel very sad. For a moment I wanted to get up and go with him. I wanted to take him in my arms and comfort him. But I didn't move. I didn't speak.

Pat stood there for a moment. Then he mumbled something I couldn't hear and walked out. I watched him go, and I felt like a hand was squeezing on my heart.

I looked up and saw Larry's blue eyes gazing at me. I felt so ashamed. "I'm sorry about that," I said. "I don't know why he—"

"Forget about it," Larry said. "It's not your fault."

But of course it was.

CHAPTER 4

When I won the lottery, I had a fantasy that I would have a closet full of beautiful suits and that each day I would put one on and go to an office job. There was more to my fantasy and not all of it came true. But I did buy three suits: a fire-engine red one, a moss green one, and a powder blue one. When I woke up the morning after my date with Larry, the date Pat had ruined, I felt that I needed to put on my red suit. I thought it would help to cheer me up. Every time I thought of Pat coming in and telling Larry I was his wife, I felt like crawling into a hole. I wasn't sure I could face Larry again. Larry had respected me. He had thought of me as a tough woman. But Pat had treated me like a naughty child, and I felt ashamed that Larry had seen that. He had probably seen the way I looked at Pat too. I wished I had no feelings for Pat, but when you have been married to someone for three years, he is under your skin. You can walk out of his house, you can divorce him, but how do you erase him from your heart?

So that's why I wanted to wear a bright red suit. But that morning, the heat was terrible. It lay over everything like a thick wool blanket. It had barely cooled off overnight. I had slept with the window wide open, yet I awoke bathed in sweat. My sheets were soaked underneath me. It was no weather for a suit, red or otherwise.

So I put on a T-shirt and shorts and sandals, swallowed a pop tart and a cup of instant coffee, and got to the office by nine. Some teenagers were coming by to pick up the posters we had made warning people to beware of Paul the Stalker. They were going to put them up around the neighborhood.

It didn't feel right sitting in the office in shorts, but our air conditioner was no match for the heat. While it was cooler inside than out, it was still very hot. I was thinking about dashing next door for a cold drink when the door opened, and Roach Roads walked in.

Outside the door, I saw his big Jaguar parked and two men sitting in it. One looked very much like Baxter.

I sat up straight in my chair and tried to control the feeling of terror that went up my spine as Roach came toward me. He had gained weight. Before he had been thin, but now he was pudgy, and his skin was a strange bluish-white. His cold little black eyes bored into me from behind his gold-rimmed glasses, and under his mustache, his lips looked very pink. Roach's hair was combed over the bald spot on the top of his head, but it had come unstuck in the heat, and I could see his scalp, covered with beads of perspiration, between the strands. He wore a light gray suit and a yellow tie.

"Good morning, Mr. Roads," I said. "May I help you?"

"Good morning, Ms. Barkin," Roach said. It was the same high, machine-like voice I remembered from before, as if Roach Roads had never felt a human emotion.

"I would like to speak with you, if I may." He sat down in the chair across from my desk. "So this is the famous W.R.C.," he said, looking around. There was a sneer in his voice. "Nobody here but you? Business must not be too good. It is not clear to me how you can make a profit on this operation."

As Roach said, 'Nobody here but you,' I heard Lech stirring under my desk. By the time Roach had finished speaking, Lech had emerged from his resting place and was standing by the desk looking at Roach. His fur was up around his neck, so I could tell he was on guard. Lech must have sensed my fear.

"And this is the famous Lech Walesa, guard dog," Roach said. A small, cruel smile appeared on his pink lips. "Never leaves your side, so I hear."

"What do you want?" I said.

"Well, I just want to tell you that I know you won $100,000 in the lottery, and I figure that the least you can do, under the circumstances, is pay it out to me."

I stared at him, speechless. My heart had begun to hammer in my chest, so loudly that I thought he must hear it. How could Roach have found out about my lottery money? Had one of my friends betrayed me? Lech growled, a low quiet growl.

"Do you understand me?" Roach Roads said.

"If I won any money, which I didn't, why would I give it to you?" I asked. My voice came out in a high little squeak.

"You know why, Ms. Barkin. You know what happens to people who cross me. And don't count on your dog. Dogs are no match for my organization." He stood up. He handed me a piece of paper. "Have the money transferred into this account. And I suggest you do it quickly." He turned and walked toward the door. Then he looked at me. "Oh, and another thing. Please stop this stupid campaign against Paul Moro. He pays me to protect him, and I consider what you are doing falls into the category of protection. Have the posters taken down and the letters and harassment stopped. Do it by tomorrow morning. If you don't, I'll send a signal to you that you will not like."

"A signal?" I said, my voice a croak.

"Yes. A signal that will give you all the more incentive to provide me with my compensation. By compensation, Ms. Barkin, I mean the lottery money. Well, I think that's all I have to say. Good-bye." He opened the door and stepped out. "I won't say good luck," he said, "because your luck has run out." Then he closed the door and walked calmly to the Jaguar. He got into the passenger seat, and the driver started up the car, backed out, and drove away.

My heart was pounding so loudly the sound seemed to fill the room. I felt as if Roach Roads's cold evil had penetrated into my flesh and was rushing through my bloodstream, poisoning me. I felt chilled too, and I realized I was shivering. If Roach had been a frightening and evil man before he went to prison, I was sure he was a hundred times worse now. His quiet politeness was more frightening to me than the loudest shouts of any other angry man. I squatted down and took Lech in my arms. He licked my face and pressed up against me. Warmth returned to my body. Strength came back into my muscles. "Thanks, Lech, I love you," I murmured into his warm fur.

I went back to my desk and sat down. I had things to do. First I called the phone company and had my telephone number at home changed to an unlisted one. I had received another of those hang-up calls last night when I got back from my "date" with Larry. And, although he had walked me home and I felt safe with him, I had felt again that weird feeling of someone following me or watching me as we walked through the neighborhood together. The phone company had my previous complaints about anonymous phone calls on file, so they agreed to give me a new unlisted number right away.

At lunchtime, Sally came by to have lunch with me and catch up on my date. She had picked up a salad for me. Sally is trying to help me stick to a diet. I don't like salad, but I appreciated the thought.

"The date was a bummer," I told Sally. "Pat wrecked it."

"Oh, no, Janet. I don't believe it," Sally said. "What happened? What did you wear? Tell me all about it."

We discussed men, clothes, and makeup for a while, but my heart wasn't in it.

"Everyone was talking about Paul Moro and our W.R.C. campaign against him at Hair-Today this morning," Sally said. "People are really down on us. They say Paul is a great guy and Nita is a flake."

"Who cares what they say?" I said. "What do they know anyway?"

"What's the matter?" Sally said. "You don't seem like yourself this morning. Are you upset about your date?"

"A little," I said. "I really like Larry Keegan, and I think Pat may have wrecked my chances with him. If I had any chances."

"Janet?" Sally said, looking at me. "Are you mad at me or something?"

"No, of course not," I said. "Why would I be?"

"Because you're acting funny, somehow."

Sally was my oldest and my best friend. Maybe I owed it to her to put my worries on the table. "Well," I said, "something happened this morning that upset me a lot."

"What happened?" Sally said. The happy, lighthearted expression vanished from her face to be replaced by an expression I knew all too well. A guilty expression.

"Roach Roads came by here," I said.

"Oh, my God!" Sally screamed. "He came here? Oh, my God, you must have been scared out of your mind!"

"Yeah, I was. He threatened me like he did before. He scared me. But that wasn't all."

"What?" Sally said. She put a finger in her mouth and nibbled on it nervously.

"He knew about the lottery money. How could he know that, Sally?"

"What are you saying?" screamed Sally. The color drained from her face. She jumped up from the chair she had been sitting on. "Are you suggesting *I* told him? I would *never never never* do that. How can you even think such a thing? I don't believe you, Janet Barkin. I DON'T BELIEVE YOU!" Tears gushed from her eyes. She turned around, rushed to the door, flung it open, and ran out, banging it behind her.

I sat there looking after her. Sally was an emotional person. She got upset easily. I could remember lots of times when she had gotten really mad at me and screamed at me and stormed out. But I saw something else in the way Sally had acted. I saw a guilty conscience.

I sat there feeling lower than a penny down a sewer grate. I tried to eat my salad but my mouth was too dry. What I needed was a chocolate doughnut. Or maybe a dozen chocolate doughnuts. Or a cigarette. Or both.

I threw my salad into the trash bin and went next door to the doughnut shop. After stocking up, I dragged myself back to the office and worked my way through the doughnuts. I didn't enjoy them, but I ate them anyway. The whole dozen.

Off and on during the afternoon, kids—friends of Porsha's—reported in. They had been following Paul and putting up posters. Their mood was not good. They said that people in the neighborhood were giving them a hard time. One even told me that someone had said that the W.R.C. was out of control. Several people had told them that since Nita was a psychic, she ought to have known better than to dump Paul. What could she expect?

By five o'clock, I had had it. I locked up the office, and Lech and I dragged ourselves home. The sidewalk was so hot I could feel it through my sandals. I noticed that several of our posters had been torn down. One poster, which said "Paul the Stalker has no respect for women," had been written over with graffiti. It now said "The W.R.C. has no respect for men." Somehow this made me feel really bad. I couldn't help but think that maybe Mrs. Gretzky and Sally had been right. Pat had told me over and over how stupid I was. He had told me the W.R.C. was a crazy idea. Maybe I should have listened.

Climbing the steps to my apartment, I felt the heat all around me, pressing down on me. As soon as Lech and I got inside, the phone began to ring. Who could it be? At least it wouldn't be the hang-up caller, I thought. After all, the phone company had changed my number right away and I hadn't given the new number to anyone yet. I had meant to tell Sally, but she had rushed out before I could.

I picked up the phone. "Hello?"

Silence.

Oh, no! It was impossible. But I recognized the familiar sound on the other end, the sound of air rushing, a faint whirring noise, and the angry, raspy breathing. I slammed down the phone. It rang again, but I did not pick it up. I looked at my dog. "Who is it, Lech?" I asked him. "Who is doing this to me?" Lech looked back at me, whining gently and wagging his tail. Obviously he didn't know either.

It was really hot. I walked slowly to the window, opened it as wide as I could, and leaned out. Not a breeze stirred. At five-thirty, the sun still shone brightly on the cars, reflecting off the metal. I looked across the street at the park. Someone waved at me. It was Pat. He sat on the bench, looking hot and miserable. I waved back. He got up and crossed the street. I ran down the stairs and let him in. He followed me up the stairs and into my apartment. I walked into the kitchen, opened the fridge, and took out two cans of Diet Coke. I handed him one. He took it and rolled it over his forehead to cool himself. Then he popped it open and drank.

Neither of us spoke. He looked as unhappy as I felt. Then he said, "I'm sorry, Janet."

"That's okay," I said, although it wasn't.

"I just hate to see you with anybody else. I lost it. I'm sorry."

"That's okay," I said again.

"Want to go out and get something to eat? We could go somewhere air-conditioned. I don't know how you stand it up here. You should at least get a fan. It's like an oven."

"I don't mind it," I said. I got up, went into my bedroom, and took a clean shirt, shorts, and underwear from the dresser. I brought them into the bathroom, showered, and changed. I felt a little better, but I also felt kind of like I was sleepwalking. What was I doing? Why had I waved to Pat to come up? Why did I feel his unhappiness was my fault and I owed him?

We walked down the stairs, Lech trailing along behind me. Pat's cell phone rang but he turned it off.

*   *   *

I awoke suddenly, my heart beating, my stomach rolling. I lurched from the bed into the bathroom and just made it before throwing up. I flushed the toilet, sat on the floor, put the lid down, and put my head on the lid. The plastic felt cool on my hot cheek. I reeked of stale beer. How many beers had I drunk? I couldn't remember. Why had I drunk them? I didn't want to remember. I hated beer. I looked at my watch. It was two A.M. It was still hot and airless.

I staggered out into the hall and looked into the bedroom. Pat lay across my bed, snoring, his skin shiny with sweat. How could I have been so stupid? I didn't want Pat back. Looking at him lying there, I knew that completely, right down in my bones. It was over between us. How could I have let him back in my bed? I would never drink another beer again.

I dragged my feet into the living room and over to the window and looked out. The street was empty. Then off in the distance, I saw headlights. A car was coming slowly along the street. As it came nearer, it turned off its headlights. It passed below my window, where I couldn't see it anymore. I heard a car door open. The sound of something being dumped. Then the car gunned its motor and sped off down the street, the car door slamming shut as it took off.

Someone had dumped something off on our doorstep. I had a bad feeling about this. Whatever had been left there, it wasn't something I wanted Mrs. Gretzky to find first.

I crept back into the bedroom and got into my clothes. Then I called quietly to Lech, and we opened the door and tiptoed down the stairs. Past the door to Porsha's apartment. Through the front hall.

I opened the front door. Something lay on the doorstep. A dark heap. I stepped back and turned on the outside light. I heard a little scream of horror. It had come from my mouth.

Nita Montez lay on my doorstep. She wore her sparkly tank top and her filmy skirt. Her black hair lay spread out around her head like a dark shadow. Nita's lovely red-lipsticked lips were open, a shocking contrast to her waxy, blue-gray skin. One side of her face was missing. Her eye, part of her nose, her ear—all gone. Part of her forehead was gone too. I could see bits of bone and pinky stuff inside. Her other eye was open and staring at me with a look of astonished terror.

Lech gave a long, eerie howl that sent a shudder up my spine. But I didn't tell him to stop because I knew how he felt, and I wanted to howl too.

CHAPTER 5

The day before, everyone had been down on the W.R.C. When we and our helpers had gone around the neighborhood saying Paul had to leave Nita alone, people had said Paul was a good guy and Nita was a flake. They were mad at us.

Now the tide had turned. Everyone was sure that Paul had killed Nita. They claimed that they had known he was crazy for love. Hadn't he talked about Romeo and Juliet? Wasn't Juliet's death all Romeo's fault? One day we are jerks, the next day heroes. It makes you wonder. And even if everyone else was now saying we tried to help Nita and were good guys, I didn't see it that way. After all, Nita was dead. I spent most of the night at the police station, giving my statement. Then I went home for a nap. By the time I got into the office, half of the day was gone.

On the office answering machine was a message from Larry, saying he was on his way over to talk to me. I had arrived just in time, for a few minutes later he turned up and we went next door to the doughnut shop for coffee.

"They put me in charge of Nita's case," Larry said. "I'm sorry, but I have to ask you some more questions."

"That's okay," I said. It really was too. Because, amazingly enough, I could tell that Larry still liked me. He still liked me, even though I had looked like a fool on our date and even though he knew that I had been with Pat when Nita's body had been dumped on my doorstep.

"I read your statement," Larry said. "Tell me again about the car. Can you remember any more? The color? The make? The size?"

I shook my head. "I really wasn't paying attention. It was so hot, and I wasn't feeling well. I only kind of half-noticed it, you know?"

"Do you think you've seen that car before?"

I thought about it. "You know," I said, "Roach Roads came around the W.R.C. office and threatened me. He said if I didn't do what he wanted, he'd send a signal. So when this happened, I thought, maybe this is Roach Roads's signal."

"Why did you think that, Janet?" Larry asked.

I shook my head in frustration. "I don't know. When you ask about the car, I wonder if it could have been that big, dark green Jaguar of his. But Paul has a 1972 Mustang. They aren't the same shape, but they are kind of the same—I don't know—bulk?"

"Well, for sure a Mustang and a Jaguar engine wouldn't sound the same," Larry said.

"I know, but I wasn't paying attention to the make or the sound. I know it's stupid. I'm sorry."

"No, no, it's not stupid," Larry said, putting his hand on mine. His touch felt wonderful. It eased my heart. "Why would you pay special attention? As far as you were concerned, it was just another car coming down the street. But why do you think Roach might have been involved? Why do you think Nita's death might be his 'signal'? What did he have to do with Nita Montez?"

"She was making trouble for Paul Moro. Or at least that's the way everyone saw it. She came to the W.R.C. to complain about him and we were . . . putting pressure on him. Paul paid protection to Roach. Paul loved Nita and he's not a murderer, no matter what everyone says. And Roach is."

Larry swore under his breath. I guess he hadn't known Roach was already back at collecting protection money from local businesses.

"Nita was shot, wasn't she?" I asked.

"Yes," Larry said. "At pretty close range. Probably by someone she knew."

"Have you talked to Paul Moro?"

"He's disappeared. Nobody has seen him since his restaurant closed last night. Nita was there, doing readings, telling fortunes. Witnesses say he asked her to stay and have a drink with him. She refused. When the last patron left, the two of them were still there, arguing—according to the patron's statement."

"What about the restaurant staff, what do they say?"

"They say Paul and Nita weren't arguing. They were having a discussion, then they walked out together. They didn't come back and the staff finished cleaning up, locked up the restaurant, and left. Paul's car was still in the lot when they left."

"Don't you think it's suspicious that Paul is missing? What if Roach killed him too?"

"Why would he do that?" Larry asked.

"I don't know," I admitted. "What about Paul's car? Did you find it in the lot?"

"No. He must have come back for it later after his staff left."

"So it could have been him," I said, not wanting to believe it. If Paul had killed Nita, I would forever wonder if we had driven him to it. On the other hand, if Roach had done it, that could be my fault too. After all, Roach had warned me to pay him my lottery money or he would send me a signal. And I hadn't paid.

"Why do you think Nita's killer dumped her body on your doorstep?" Larry asked.

"Nita came to me—to the W.R.C.—for help," I said. "Everyone knew that. We tried to help her the best way we could. What we did made a lot of people mad at us. Maybe someone wants to send a message that bad things will happen to anyone who comes to the W.R.C. for help. Maybe someone wants to put us out of business."

"What you did wasn't too popular, that's for sure," Larry said. "Nita was a beautiful, sexy woman. People thought she should take it in stride if a man was crazy in love with her. They thought she must have done something to make him act like that."

"I hate that idea," I said. "I don't think a man has a right to stalk a woman and ruin her life if she decides to leave him."

"Do you think you guys had a right to stalk him back?" Larry said. His clear blue eyes looked into mine.

"I don't know!" I cried. "What else could we do? Was she supposed to put up with it? With having her life ruined?"

"It's a tough call, Janet," Larry said. "But somehow, the murderer blames you. I guess that points to either Paul or Roach."

"Well, you'll find Paul. Where can he go? The police are looking for him, aren't they? You'll talk to him, get his side of the story?"

"Right," Larry said.

"And Roach? Have you brought him in for questioning?" I asked.

"Of course. But he came with his lawyer. And you know how slick Roach is. We can't prove any link between Nita and Roach."

"What about what Roach said to me? About sending a signal?" I asked. "What about his threats?"

"We have nothing concrete," Larry said. "You don't arrest someone because he says he is going to send a signal. We'd all like to see Roach back behind bars, but getting him for this murder? I don't think so. No motive, and Roach has an alibi. An employee of his, Baxter, said Roach was with him that evening."

"Baxter!" I said. "Baxter is working for Roach again?"

Larry nodded and I saw he had told me this for a reason. He knew about Sally and Baxter. He knew I loved Sally. Probably he wanted me to warn Sally. I couldn't believe Sally knew Baxter was working for Roach. After all, Roach was a murderer. He had tried to kill me before he went to jail and was threatening to do so again. Surely Sally wouldn't stay with Baxter knowing he was working for Roach?

I saw that Larry was looking at me with tenderness and concern. He was watching as the significance of his words sank in.

"I have to go now," I said.

Larry stood up. "Janet," he said. "I care about you. I know you have to do what you have to do. But be careful. Roach is angrier than ever with you. He didn't enjoy being forced to come to the police station and answer questions. He blames you. And no one knows where Paul is or what he might do."

"I understand," I said.

I stood up and we looked at each other. Then he gave me a quick hug. I'm sure he meant it as a friendly hug, but it turned into something more, and we both felt it.

We stepped apart. "I've got to go," I said. "Come on, Lech." I grabbed my purse and left the office. Outside on the sidewalk stood Pat. Again. Why was he around so much? He never used to be.

"What are you doing here?" I said to him rudely. I was fed up with him. I had told him I never wanted to see him again, but every time I turned around, there he was. I had told him our night together was a mistake. He had just smiled. But he wasn't smiling now.

"I saw that!" he said. "I saw you and him. I saw what you did just now!"

"Oh, leave me alone!" I shouted. I took off down the street, Lech scampering along at my side.

The sky had clouded over. It was still hot, but without the sun beating down, it didn't feel as bad as it had for the last few days. Occasional gusts of wind blew scraps of paper and grit up into the air. The city seemed to be suspended in a dull haze of heat. In the distance, I thought I heard the low rumble of thunder.

I walked and walked, Lech at my side, thinking about everything that had happened. The hang-up phone calls and my sense of being spied on and followed. Nita's plea for help, the W.R.C. campaign against Paul, and then Nita's murder. The poisoned meat meant for Lech that had killed the stray dog. Sally's boyfriend Baxter working for Roach Roads. Roach's threats. Romeo and Juliet. My attraction for Larry Keegan, and Pat's weird behavior. Pat had been getting worse and worse. Somehow it was hard for him that I had been on TV and worked at the W.R.C., and his job as an undercover cop didn't seem to be going anywhere. Larry Keegan was sent on a course at Quantico run by the F.B.I., and Pat had to hang out on the other side of town, spying on small-time drug dealers. My thoughts went round and round and nothing seemed to fit together or make sense. One thing was clear: we had failed Nita. She had come to us for help and now she was dead.

I got back to the office to find Porsha, Sally, and Mrs. Gretzky waiting for me. Because of Nita's connection to the W.R.C., everyone had been required to give statements to the police. Now they sat in the office looking glum.

I sat down and looked around. The faces of my friends reflected the same grief and sadness I felt.

I filled them in on everything Larry had told me. About Paul and Nita's discussion—or argument. About them leaving the restaurant together and about Paul being missing.

"Paul is the key to everything," Porsha said. "We've got to find that Romeo. Talk to him. Look him in the eye and say to him, 'Okay, man, what's your story?'"

"If the police can't find him, how can we?" Sally said. She didn't look at me. I couldn't look at her either. How could I doubt my best friend? And how could I trust her when she was back with Baxter—who was working for Roach?

"People don't tell the police much," Mrs. Gretzky said. "You can't trust them. Cops say things to get you to do what they want. Then they change their tune." Mrs. Gretzky had friends among a lot of the old people in the neighborhood. I knew if any of them had seen Paul, they might not tell the cops, but they'd tell Mrs. Gretzky.

"Come on," I said. "Larry Keegan is a good guy."

"I know two kids who work as busboys at Paul's Steakhouse," Porsha said. "I can find out what happened between Nita and Paul last night. Bet you anything they didn't tell the cops the whole story."

"I could talk to Nita's sister, Carmen," I said. "I called her this morning to offer my sympathies, and I promised I would come over this afternoon. I bet she can tell me stuff about Paul . . . places he might go. Carmen and Nita were very close." I looked at Sally. "Sally, you better talk to Baxter. See if he knows anything."

Sally looked down at her hands. Her fingernails were perfect. She wore dark red nail polish and she had a tiny jewel stuck into one fingernail. "I don't know if I can do that," Sally said. She spoke so softly I wasn't sure if I heard her correctly.

"What?" I said.

Sally put both hands over her ears and squinched up her eyes. "I'm scared of what he'll do if I ask him. He's been acting awfully strange lately. I said something about Roach, and he got really upset with me."

Baxter could be violent. I thought Sally should leave him. But I knew it would do no good to say so.

"You know, guys," I said, "you were right and I was wrong. It was a mistake to hassle Paul. We acted just like he did. It was wrong when he acted that way and wrong when the W.R.C. gave him a taste of his own medicine. Sally had a bad feeling about that plan and Mrs. Gretzky did too. They were right. Porsha, you and I should have listened to them."

Porsha nodded. "I guess so," she said. "But it seemed like a good idea at the time."

"We need to make it up to him," I said. "If he killed Nita, then of course, he's responsible and he has to pay the price. But if he didn't, we owe him an apology and help in clearing his name."

"I can't agree with that," Porsha said. "No way do we apologize to Romeo. He hassled and followed Nita. He probably killed her too."

"And," I continued, "right now the W.R.C. is looking bad. Someone came to us for help and ended up dead. We've got to find out who killed Nita and why. We need to do whatever it takes. And we have no proof it was Paul. Until we do, we shouldn't blame him. Okay?" I looked around. Everyone nodded their agreement.

Sally said, "Janet, you're so brave. People threaten you and you just keep going. But I'm just not like that. I'm scared. I know Baxter's mixed up in all this somehow, but he doesn't tell me anything. And if I ask him . . ." She buried her face in her hands. "I'm just too scared to."

I got up and went over to Sally and put my arms around her. "It's okay," I said. "We're going to find out what is going on. You're going to help. Keep an eye on Baxter. And if you ever need to get away, you know you can come to my place. Lech will never let anyone hurt you."

Sally looked up. Her eyes glistened with tears. "I won't let you down, Janet," she said. "I promise."

CHAPTER
6

Nita's sister, Carmen, opened the door and out burst the sound of a baby screaming at the top of its lungs.

"Janet! Come in, come in, I'm just feeding the baby," Carmen said, and without waiting for an answer, she disappeared back inside her house.

I followed.

Carmen lived in a subdivision in Deerfield, a town north of Evanston. I had borrowed an old clunker from a friend of Mrs. Gretzky's and had driven out. My timing was lousy. I got caught in rush hour traffic, it began to rain, and I was half an hour later than I'd said I'd be.

I found Carmen in the kitchen. The baby was in a highchair. She had huge, soft brown eyes, black hair sticking up in tufts, and a face covered with bright green goop. Her mouth was wide open and Carmen sat beside the highchair, shoveling in more green goop from a baby

51

food jar. Everytime she paused, the kid screamed. While her mouth was open, Carmen would stuff another spoonful in.

A toddler was crawling around the floor. When he saw Lech follow me in, he began to scream too. "Mama! Mama! A doggie! Mama! Dog bite me! Eeeeee! Bad doggie!"

"Jesus," Carmen said. She stopped feeding the baby and scooped up the toddler, dropping him into a playpen that stood in the middle of the kitchen. The playpen was full of toys. The toddler began to fling them at Lech. "Go away, doggie!" the toddler yelled. "Bad doggie! Out out out!"

The baby in the highchair opened her mouth and out came a wave of green goop. It rolled down her face and dripped onto the highchair tray.

"I'm sorry," Carmen said. "You must be disgusted." She took up a handful of paper towels, wet them, and began to wipe the baby's face.

"No, *I'm* sorry," I said. "I see I've come at a bad time. Anything I can do to help?"

"Yes, please, can you put your dog in the car or something? Sean is terrified of dogs."

I walked Lech out and told him to wait by the front door. When I returned to the kitchen, the toddler was jumping up and down inside the playpen, crying to be let out. The baby had a cookie in a fat fist and was mashing it against her gums and making slurping noises.

"Do you think any of that spinach stayed inside or did Lucinda spit it all up?" Carmen asked me, a worried look on her face.

"Lucinda is the baby?" I asked.

Carmen smiled for the first time and brushed some hair off her face. She sighed, picked the toddler up out of the playpen, and sat down at the kitchen table, the kid on her lap. She pointed to the chair opposite. I sat down across from her. "This is Sean. Say hello to the nice lady, Sean."

Sean turned his face away from me and buried it in his mother's chest.

"Sean is three. Lucinda is nine months," Carmen said.

"Sean a good boy but Luci a bad girl," Sean said, lifting his head and sticking a finger in his ear. "Luci throw up her supper. Yucky poo-poo."

Carmen gently removed the little boy's finger from his ear and hugged him. I noticed that her eyes were swollen and red.

"I'm so sorry about Nita," I said.

"You tried to help her, and we are all grateful," Carmen said. She had thick black hair like her sister's, but hers was cut short. Carmen was bigger than her sister and not as glamorous, but she had the same warm, gentle voice.

"I told Nita that Paul would never leave his wife," Carmen said. "I told her to break up with him. For a long time, she just couldn't do it. Maybe she saw something in the stars. Ever since she was little, Nita had the second sight. Some people laughed at her, but it was true. You know that, Janet."

"Yes," I said.

"She told me everything. When she fell in love with Paul, she told me. She knew it was wrong, a married man and all, but he swept her off her feet. You know how he could be."

"I know she loved him," I said. "But then she stopped."

"She felt so guilty. He had a wife, kids. And then he was so—possessive. He wouldn't leave her any space. He tried to control everything she did. What she wore. Who she talked to. Even what she thought. If she expressed her own opinion and it was different from his, he told her she was stupid."

"I've been there," I said.

For a moment, both Carmen and I were silent.

"Do you think he killed her?" I asked Carmen.

Carmen hugged her little boy harder. He squirmed out from her arms and slid down from the chair. He toddled out of the kitchen and disappeared into the living room.

I looked at the baby. She was rubbing what was left of her spit-soaked cookie into her hair and seemed quite happy. Cookie chunks and spinach baby food were spattered on the floor all around the highchair.

"I can't believe Paul would kill her," Carmen said. "I just can't." Her big dark eyes, so like her sister's, looked incredibly sad. "He loved her. How is it possible? He said he couldn't live without her. If he killed her, then—he'd never have her. It doesn't make any sense."

"Have you seen him or talked to him since she died?" I asked.

Carmen didn't answer. She got up and went over to the baby. She gently washed the baby's face and cleaned her hair. Then she wiped up the highchair and the floor. She found a box of baby cookies and handed the baby another cookie. The baby immediately mashed the cookie into her mouth.

"Carmen?" I said.

Carmen came back and sat across from me. "I didn't tell the police this. Do you promise not to tell?"

"What?" I asked.

"Paul came here this morning. He was in bad shape. He just sat there," Carmen pointed to where I was sitting, "and he hardly talked at all. Then he asked me if I would go for a ride with him in his Mustang. He had the top down. It was a ridiculous question. I have two little kids—I can't go out joyriding in a convertible. Anyway, it looked like rain."

"Did he say where he was going when he left?"

"Listen, Janet, I didn't tell the police he came here, okay? I lied and said I hadn't seen him. Please don't tell them."

"Why, Carmen? Why did you lie?"

"I don't know!" Carmen said. She twisted her hands together. "There was something about the way Paul looked . . . the way he acted." She jumped up suddenly. "How come it's so quiet in the living room? What is that kid up to?" She rushed into the living room, and at the same time I heard a crash and the sound of breaking glass.

"Jesus, Sean!" Carmen shouted from the living room. "How did you get up there? Haven't I told you and told you not to climb on the furniture! Bad boy! You broke my ballerina! Now you are going to your room." Screams and howls of *no, no*, faded away, and then I heard a door slam. The howls continued, but they were muffled.

Carmen came back and collapsed into her chair. "I can't believe that kid. He's like a monkey. He climbed up on the shelves and broke a beautiful china ballerina Nita gave me for my birthday."

I don't know how people with kids do it. Carmen looked like she might not know either.

"Did Paul say where he was going?" I asked Carmen.

"He left a note for you, Janet," Carmen said.

"He what?" This didn't make any sense. How did Paul know I would come to see Carmen? "Why would he leave me a note?" I asked Carmen.

"He talked about you. How everything was your fault. He said you made Nita hate him."

"That's not fair!" I said.

"I know, I know, I tried to tell him but he wouldn't listen. I told him how you called here to offer your sympathies, how sweet you were. How you were coming over today—remember, you said you would when you called? I told him if he'd only give you a chance, talk to you, it might comfort him."

"Thanks a lot," I said.

"He waited for a while in case you came by. Then he said he had to go and he left you this."

Carmen got up, crossed the kitchen, and opened a drawer. She handed me a piece of paper. I unfolded it. It was a note written on notepaper with *Paul's Steakhouse* at the top. In heavy black ink, in an angry slashing handwriting, Paul had written:

Janet,

I need to talk to you. This is all your fault. Meet me at the Bridge over Troubled Waters.

—Paul

Below this scrawl Paul had sketched out a map.

I looked up at Carmen. "He says he's going to the Bridge over Troubled Waters. What's that?"

"It's a place they used to go to talk. It's a bridge over a stream in the forest preserve. Kind of a secret place. When they first fell in love, it used to be their special place. Nita said that there were good spirits in the water there to soothe a troubled heart."

"I guess you didn't tell the police about this."

"No. I thought Paul had a right to some time in peace at the bridge."

"You're not afraid of him?"

Carmen shook her head, but I thought she wasn't being completely truthful with herself or with me. I thought Carmen was afraid of Paul, afraid of that crazy look he could get, afraid to tell the cops where he had gone, afraid to get him in trouble. She was telling me instead, so Paul wouldn't take revenge on her if something bad happened.

"Could you show me where it is? Where this bridge is?"

"Sorry, but I can't get away. As soon as Dan comes home, I'm going over to Mom's. Mom really needs me right now."

"Well," I said, "he drew me a map. I guess I can find it."

I said good-bye to Carmen, tucked the map into my purse, and left. Outside, it was raining heavily. As Lech and I got into the car, I heard a loud peal of thunder, and lightning flashed across the sky. It was almost seven o'clock, but darker than usual, because of the heavy black clouds. Yet it was still too warm. Miserable weather.

I drove through the rain to the forest preserve and parked. Paul's sketch showed a path that wandered through the woods along a stream. I found it and started walking. By the time I saw the little bridge in the distance, I was soaked through.

The forest preserve must have been very beautiful on a nice day, but in the rain and wind it seemed dark and scary. Lech moved along beside me, dripping and shivering in the rain. The trees shook and bent over me as I walked, and the path turned to mud under my feet. The stream ran swiftly between its banks, the deep water dark brown with leaves and mud.

The little bridge was made of wood with high wooden railings. I stood for a moment, imagining a sunny day, Paul and Nita in love, standing on the bridge, maybe throwing pennies into the stream and making wishes.

Love is a funny thing. You can't control who you fall in love with or when you fall out. You can't control the strange things love makes you want to do. But while feelings can be out of control, you still have to take responsibility for your actions.

The rain pelted down harder, streaming over my eyes. Surely Paul wouldn't be here anymore. He had left the map with Carmen hours before. And if he was here, why would I want to meet an angry, half-crazy man in the middle of nowhere? I should leave. Forget about the bridge. But I kept on walking.

I wiped my eyes with the bottom of my T-shirt and approached the bridge. Through the downpour I saw a shadowy figure standing in the middle of it, a white face looking back at me through the rain.

"Janet? Is that you?" a voice called out to me from the bridge.

"Paul?" I called back.

"Janet? Are you alone?"

"Just me and Lech," I called back.

A shot rang out.

The figure on the bridge fell forward, collapsing upon the floor of the bridge.

I dropped to my knees and looked around. There was no one in sight. The rain poured down; the wind rushed through the trees with a moaning sound. My heart banged in my chest while I awaited the second shot. But nothing happened.

No one shot at me.

I looked at Lech. He was staring at the bridge, his fur soggy, his ears alert. I could see that he was not on guard. He was acting as if there was nothing to fear.

The man on the bridge might need my help! Without

further thought, I stood up and ran to the bridge, to the man lying sprawled there. I looked down.

It was Paul.

Blood flowed from his head and pooled under it. Just like Nita, half his face had been shot off. The rain poured down on him, and even as I watched, the blood on the wound washed away to reveal white bone poking out of the black hole in the side of his face.

I realized I was shaking and I heard my teeth chatter. I knew I should feel fear. Whoever had shot Paul must be near. He might be in the woods right now with a gun trained on me. But Lech's calm communicated itself to me.

The smart thing to do would be to get out of there, but instead I told Lech to stand back and guard the bridge. Walking around Paul's body, careful not to touch anything, I looked for the gun. Had Paul shot himself or had someone killed him? I hadn't seen anyone else. Lech hadn't sensed anyone else. Could Paul have waited until he saw me, then fired the gun into his own head? But if he had done that, where was the gun?

I examined the bridge carefully. It was old and in places rotten boards had been patched, but it was solid. There was no way a gun could have fallen through the planks or slid off the bridge into the water. Near where Paul lay, there was a fresh chip on the outer edge of the bridge and scratches on the railing. If Paul had shot himself, could the gun have fallen from his hand and slid into the water? I didn't think so. Even if the gun had slid from his hand as he fell, it could not have fallen off the bridge. It would have been caught by the mesh that had been installed between the railing and floor of the bridge—obviously to make it safer for children.

No matter who had shot Paul, one thing was certain. Now both Romeo and Juliet were dead.

CHAPTER 7

"Tell me again what happened," Larry asked.

Larry sat across from me at the police station. His eyes were rimmed with red, and his face looked as exhausted as I felt.

After reporting that Paul had been shot, I had spent hours at the police station making a statement. I had talked to an officer I did not know, then to Larry, then to the strange officer again. Just when I thought we were all finished, the police officer left the room and Larry came in. Without saying hello, he sat down across from me.

I was dead tired. It was the middle of the night. My clothes were still damp, and I shivered in the air-conditioned police interview room. I missed Lech. Larry had asked one of his friends to take Lech home and leave him with Mrs. Gretzky. Did that mean I was about to be arrested? Larry was acting strange. Cold. Distant.

"What happened?" Larry repeated. "Tell me one more time."

I sighed. I had told my story over and over. Each time I told it, it sounded more unbelievable. I said, "I went to the bridge. I saw someone standing there. He called out to me. I answered. Then I heard a shot. I ran to him. He was dead—shot through the head. As soon as I was sure he was dead, I got out of there, went to the nearest pay phone, and called 911."

Larry sighed. He handed me a sheet of paper and asked, "Did you write this letter?"

I looked at the paper. It was a computer printout. It read:

Dear Paul:

I am sorry that you failed to listen when I explained to you that you must leave Nita Montez alone. You failed to appreciate the pain and suffering you are causing her by your unwanted attentions.

No man has the right to pursue a woman who does not wish to be pursued.

No man has the right to harass and follow and pester a woman who has told him she never wishes to see him again.

The W.R.C. was founded to help women in trouble. You are causing trouble to Nita. We have warned you to stop and you have paid no attention.

You must stop or we will stop you.

You have been warned. Heed our warning or you will suffer the consequences.

Beware!

Sincerely yours,

Janet Barkin

Janet Barkin for the W.R.C.

I read the letter twice. My mind was numb. I didn't know what to say. "Where did you find this letter?" I asked Larry.

"Please answer the question, Janet," Larry said. "Did you write it?"

"No . . . yes . . . it's not that simple!"

"Either you wrote it or you didn't. Answer the question."

Now I was getting mad. "Okay. Be that way. I didn't write it."

"Is that your signature?" Larry demanded.

"Yes and no."

"Janet . . ." He was mad now.

"It's my signature because that's how I sign letters and that's the way I write my signature, but I didn't sign that letter."

"Who did?"

"I don't know."

Larry stared at me, trying to figure out what was going on. "Have you seen this letter before?" he asked.

"No."

Larry sighed. He got up and walked around. We were in a small room with a mirror on one side, a scratched table, and old chairs. A tape recorder was running. Larry had read me the warning about anything you say being used against you. He had asked if I wanted a lawyer and I had said no. That was because I trusted Larry. Or at least, I *had* trusted him, until he pulled the letter on me. Where had he found it?

"What can you tell me about this letter, Janet?" Larry said.

"First you tell me where you found it."

"When you and I are in this room," Larry said, "I ask the questions and you answer them."

"Then I won't answer," I said.

"Jeez, Janet," Larry said in exasperation. "I'm trying to help you here. But you are not making it any easier. I'm just trying to find out what happened. How come the police of four counties are looking for Paul Moro, and you get in a car and drive out to a deserted forest preserve and see him shot before your eyes?"

"Do you think I shot him?"

"I told you, I ask the questions here," Larry said again, his voice angry, his face cold.

"That bridge was a favorite meeting spot of Nita and Paul. I thought he might go there to remember her. He was that kind of guy," I said. I know it was stupid, but I was so tired, I completely forgot about the note from Paul in my purse. The note with the map of the bridge's location.

"Who told you it was a favorite meeting place?" Larry asked.

Then I remembered. "Oh, my God, the note," I said. "I can explain—"

"Yes. The note in your purse. The note from Paul inviting you to the bridge. I have the note, Janet. Looks like he invited you to meet him there and then he got shot."

"You know I didn't do it!" I said. I looked at Larry to see if he believed me. I could hardly think anymore. But even tired and numb as I was, I knew it looked bad. A letter to Paul signed by me that sounded like a threat. A note from him telling me where he was, a note I had "forgotten" to mention. My saying I saw him shot before my eyes. If I heard that story, I wouldn't believe it. Come to think of it, it was surprising I wasn't already arrested. It was all so strange. Like a nightmare. I felt as if all the bad things that had been happening—the hang-up calls, the poisoned dog, Roach Roads's threats, Paul's craziness—had been leading up to this. To my being arrested for a murder I didn't do.

Larry said, "Are you sure you didn't see anybody else there? Or hear anybody running away?"

It almost sounded as if Larry was pleading with me. As if he wanted to me to lie.

"No," I said. "But I had a creepy feeling like I was being watched. That doesn't mean anything, though. I've been getting that feeling for weeks. And somebody tried to poison Lech."

"Come on, Janet. I know you're hiding things. If you didn't write that letter to Paul, who did? It's signed 'for the W.R.C.' Did one of your friends write it and sign it for you?"

"Where did you find that letter?" I repeated. I had to know.

"Okay," Larry said. "We found the letter from you in Paul's pocket. Help me here, Janet. It doesn't look good for you. Whatever happened, I know you, I know you didn't mean to hurt him."

"I didn't kill him!" I said.

"You were mad at him. You threatened him. You thought he killed Nita and dumped her on your doorstep to show you it was your fault. You tried writing letters and that didn't work. You thought he had no right to stalk Nita and yet nothing you could do would stop him. I can understand how frustrated you felt. Then he invited you out to a lonely spot and threatened you. You argued with him. He came at you and you shot him in self-defense. You can tell me about it, Janet," Larry said, leaning forward and looking sympathetically at me. "I'll understand."

"Oh, get real, that's ridiculous," I said. But I said it weakly. I couldn't get any anger into my voice because I did feel as if I had killed Paul Moro. And Nita too. After all, would either Romeo or Juliet be dead if it weren't for their feuding families? And just as the families of Romeo and Juliet had caused their deaths, maybe the W.R.C. had brought about the deaths of Paul and Nita. Why had I thought I could help? Why had I gotten mixed up in it? I put my hand to my face. It was wet, and I realized that I was crying.

"I can't say anything else," I said. "I need to talk to my buddies at the W.R.C. first." I looked at my watch. "It's two in the morning, Larry. I'm beat. And Lech needs a walk. How about I go home and tomorrow I talk to my friends at the W.R.C. Then we can talk again and I'll answer the rest of your questions about the letter, okay?"

"You got it," Larry said, surprising me completely. "Let me take you home." He turned off the tape. We left the interview room, walked through the station, and went out the front door.

It was dark and so late that there was hardly any traffic. The streets were quiet and the air was cool. The rain had stopped, but the pavements were still wet and when a car went by, it made a swishing sound as the tires passed over the road. "My car is around the back," Larry said.

As soon as we were behind the station, Larry took me in his arms. We clutched one another. "I wanted to hold you in there," Larry whispered. "It tears me up to see you cry. But that mirror, it's one-way glass and someone might have been watching. Are you okay?"

"No," I said. I pressed my head into his shoulder. I loved the feeling of his arms around me. How I wanted his comfort. But I was still afraid to trust him. Inside the police station he had been trying to make me confess to a murder. Okay, he was just doing his job, but that didn't change things. Right now I was the best suspect to have murdered Paul Moro.

"How come you haven't arrested me?" I murmured, pressing my face into his shoulder.

Larry held me tighter. "I know you, Janet. You are brave and good. This whole thing doesn't sit right. I've seen you under pressure. Shooting Paul, no, that's not you."

For a moment, joy surged through me. I let myself feel his respect and his trust. But then I remembered my situation. I remembered the words Larry had spoken to me in the interview room while other policemen watched through the one-way glass and the tape recorder recorded. Larry might believe me, but no one else would.

Even as Larry held me in his arms, I knew I did not dare to tell him everything. Suppose he really did care for me? Suppose because of that, he figured it couldn't have been me who fired the fatal shot? Then he might decide one of the other W.R.C. women had done it. What if he knew Carmen had had the note saying Paul was going to the Bridge over Troubled Waters? Larry might suspect Carmen. She would have good reason to want to kill the man everyone thought murdered her sister. I couldn't take the chance.

And there was more.

The police records showed that I owned a gun. Pat had gotten one for me and taught me how to shoot it. But I had always hated it. As soon as I left Pat, I got rid of the gun. But I couldn't prove that. And when Larry had asked me to produce my gun, I had had to admit that I didn't have it and didn't know where it was. I couldn't remember. Had I given it away or had I just left it behind when I moved out on Pat? That was a bad time for me, and there was much about it I couldn't remember. But I was not sure that Larry believed me when I said I didn't know what had happened to my gun.

I watched Larry's face as he drove the car toward my

place. I could see he was thinking hard. A couple of times he sighed. Larry was worried. But no matter how bad he felt, he couldn't feel nearly as bad as I did. I kept seeing Paul lying there, blood flowing from his head. Over and over I heard in my imagination the sound of the shot, ringing out in the dark woods.

"We looked for the gun in the stream under the bridge," Larry said suddenly.

"Did you find it?" I asked.

"No," Larry said. "But now that the rain has stopped, the water will be clearer. We'll try again. The stream has a gravel bottom and it is not very deep. If the gun is down there, we'll find it tomorrow."

I wondered if Larry was letting me go home while he waited to see if they could find the gun. If they did, and it was Paul's, they might decide that Paul had shot himself and dropped the gun over the railing, no matter how impossible that seemed. If the gun belonged to someone else, I might be okay. But if it was mine, they would have to arrest me. Even Larry couldn't protect me then. But of course, there was no way that could happen. No way. If only I knew where my gun was!

We got to my apartment and I reached out to open the car door.

"Janet . . ." Larry said, his voice very soft.

I turned to him. "What?"

He looked at me and I saw that he wanted to hold me again. Instead he said, "Don't get me in trouble, please. Don't do anything tomorrow except talk to your friends. Then come over to the station, okay?"

"I promise," I said.

I got out of the car. He waited until I was inside. Then I heard him drive off.

I picked up Lech from Mrs. Gretzky, took him for a quick walk, then staggered upstairs and collapsed on my bed. I was so tired I could barely find the energy to take off my still-damp clothes and get into a dry T-shirt. Yet I couldn't sleep. For the rest of the night my thoughts raced in my head, and even though my apartment was hot and stuffy, I shivered and could not get warm.

CHAPTER 8

I awoke with a start. I must have fallen asleep at dawn because I remember the sky getting pink as I drifted off. Now bright, hot sunlight was pouring in through the open window. The sky was a brilliant blue with small, puffy white clouds in it.

I got up, took a shower, and made myself some coffee. I slathered my pop tarts with jam. I needed a good sugar rush for the day ahead. While I ate, Lech lay on the floor in the living room, watching cartoons on TV, his favorite thing.

As soon as I was done eating, I called to him and told him we had to get going. He looked up at me and I saw he was peeved. He was watching *101 Dalmatians, The Series*, his favorite show. He banged his tail on the floor and stuck his nose between his paws, letting me know he didn't want to leave while his show was on.

"Come on, Lech," I said. "I'm sorry, but we have to go

meet the guys at the W.R.C., and then I have to go to the police station. I don't have time to wait around." I turned off the TV.

Lech got up slowly. His disgusted look said, "After all I've done for you, I don't even get to watch my favorite show!"

"Sorry about that," I said as we went down the stairs. "I'll make it up to you, as soon as I find out the truth about Paul's death." Lech made a kind of snorting noise. Obviously he didn't think I had much chance of solving the mystery. Or maybe he was still upset about missing the end of his show.

Outside it was bright and warm but not nearly as hot as it had been. The rain must have cooled the air. Lech trotted along beside me, looking from side to side. I wondered if he was watching out for the person I had sensed following me over the past week or so. I looked too, but I couldn't see anything except the usual people and cars.

As soon as I opened the door to the W.R.C. office, everyone screamed. "Janet!" They rushed over to me and hugged me. "We were so scared they were going to arrest you," Sally said.

"You okay?" Porsha wanted to know.

"You poor thing," Mrs. Gretzky murmured as she hugged me.

We pulled our chairs into a circle and sat down. I repeated to everyone what had happened the day before. They already knew part of it from the gossip going around. They knew how I had discovered Paul's body, driven to the nearest telephone, and called the cops. They knew I had been taken in for questioning and had been at the police station until the middle of the night. I filled them in on how Paul was shot, and then I told them about the W.R.C. letter found in his pocket.

"Sounds like one I wrote," Porsha said.

"I signed your name to all the letters Porsha printed out of the computer, just like you told me," Sally said.

"One of the kids probably took it over to Paul's restaurant," Porsha said. "I don't see the big deal about it being in his pocket. We must have sent that guy thirty letters. Everyone knew we were doing that."

"The big deal is that it was in his pocket the day he was shot," I said. "It looks like a threat from me. Even like maybe I sent it, then met him at the bridge and shot him. He left Carmen a note telling me to meet him at the bridge. I put it in my purse and the police found it. That was weird. Why would he ask me to meet him at the bridge?"

"You sure the note was from Paul?" Sally asked. "It sounds like someone was trying to get you in trouble. You know, get you and Paul to the bridge and once you were there, shoot Paul and you get blamed."

"It's so crazy!" I said. "Carmen said the note was from Paul. From the notepaper and the handwriting, it sure looked like it was. Why would Carmen lie?"

"Do you trust her?" Sally asked.

"Yes, I do," I said.

"This whole thing, Paul sending you the note and getting shot when you got there hours later, it doesn't fit together," Porsha said. "You certain he couldn't have done it himself?"

"I don't see how," I said uneasily. "There was no gun there."

"He shot himself and with his dying gasp, he flung it from the bridge?" Porsha said.

Mrs. Gretzky shook her head. "I've seen people shot," she said. "It doesn't go like that. Shot in the head, you say, Janet? Well, if he did that, if he shot himself in the head, then his fingers might tighten on the gun and he'd still have it. Maybe the gun would fall from his hand. You would see it next to him. Or maybe under him. But he couldn't throw it anywhere."

Mrs. Gretzky didn't talk about her life in Poland before she came to America. But I knew she had lived through the second World War. I was not surprised to hear she had seen someone shot.

"Where he was lying, I don't see how the gun could have fallen off the bridge if he shot himself and then dropped it," I said.

"How high was the railing?" Porsha asked.

"Chest high," I said. "I didn't tell Larry Keegan you wrote the letter, Porsha, though I figured you did. But I don't want to get you in trouble."

"I don't care," Porsha said. "Tell him the truth."

But of course, she did care. Porsha couldn't afford to get in trouble. She wanted to get a scholarship to go to college. Her mother worked two jobs and Porsha was totally set on going to college and being a lawyer. When I saw how smart Porsha was and what a great kid she was, I wanted to do everything I could to help her achieve her goal. No way would I rat on her.

"You may have typed the words into the computer, Porsha," I said. "But the idea of the letters was mine. So I think it's more true to say that I wrote the letter."

"Wait a minute—" Porsha began.

"That's not right!" Sally interrupted.

"Don't ask for trouble," Mrs. Gretzky said.

"It's all of us," Sally said. "You tell Larry Keegan we wrote the letters together and we sent them together, you hear?"

We argued for some time, and in the end they made it clear that they wouldn't let me take responsibility for the letter alone. I didn't think it would make any difference. If the police decided I killed Paul, they could use the letter in court. It had my name on it.

"By the way, Janet," Porsha said. "I made that tape for you." She handed me a little cassette tape, the kind that goes into an answering machine. "It's really gruesome. A friend of mine has stuff on his computer to mix sound. I made an extra copy for Halloween."

"What's on the tape?" Sally asked.

I didn't answer. The tape was a secret plan of mine, and I didn't want to tell anyone else about it. It was no big deal and probably didn't have anything to do with the W.R.C.'s activities anyway.

I held it in my hand. For a moment I thought of giving it back to Porsha. I had had the idea about the tape before Paul was shot. Did I really want to continue fighting back? Look what had happened when we tried to stand up for Nita. Everyone said women just had to take it.

No, I couldn't live like that. I remembered when I had been afraid of everything and had lived by the motto *Don't make waves*. I never wanted to be that cowardly woman again.

I took the tape and put it in my purse. "Did you talk to your friends who bus at Paul's Steakhouse?" I asked Porsha.

"Yes, " Porsha said. "They told me Paul and Nita had a really bad argument, and they were still fighting when they left the restaurant the night she was shot."

"What were they fighting about?" I asked.

"He wanted her back, and she told him it would never, never happen. He seemed to think if she wouldn't go back, she must be seeing someone else. He kept asking her who her new lover was. My friends say Paul was, like, really, really upset. He told her she was his, and nobody else would ever have her. He said he would find out who her new lover was and he would kill him."

"And they call that love?" Mrs. Gretzky said. "Didn't I tell you? Life is hard."

"I better get over to the police station like I promised," I said. I handed Porsha the W.R.C. credit card. "Porsha, could you buy us a cell phone?"

Everyone looked at me. I knew they were thinking we didn't need a cell phone. We had all agreed that we would run the W.R.C. as cheaply as we could. We wanted my lottery money to last as long as possible. "I have some things to do in the next few days," I said. "I'm going to need it. But I think it would be best to put it in the name of the W.R.C."

"Janet, if you have a plan, you've got to tell us the rest of us," Porsha said. "That's the deal."

"I wish I had a plan," I said. "I just have a sort of skinny little idea."

We talked a little more, dividing up the work that needed to be done. Then I called to Lech, and he crawled out from under my desk. Together we headed over to the police station.

Larry was there, looking, if possible, even more tired than the night before. He led me back to the same room I had been in the previous day.

We both sat down. Larry sighed. He turned on the tape recorder and gave me the warning again.

As soon as he was done, I said. "Did you find the gun that shot Paul?"

Larry leaned back in his chair and put his hands behind his head. "No," he said. "The stream water level has gone down enough so we could do a really good search this morning. The gun is not anywhere near the bridge."

"So it's murder," I said. I shivered. Larry's news meant the murderer had been near when I saw Paul on the bridge. The murderer must have heard Paul call out to me. He could have shot me easily if he had wanted to. But it seemed he didn't want to.

"It looks like murder," Larry agreed.

"Are you going to arrest me?" I asked. My heart had begun to beat rapidly in my chest. I wished I had Lech near me, but they were looking after him in the reception area of the station. What a stupid thought. Did I think Lech could protect me from being arrested?

"There's something else," Larry said. He ran his hand over his face, and then he rubbed his eyes. "The bullet that killed Paul matches the one that killed Nita. They were shot with the same gun."

"So that's why you think I didn't do it?"

Larry looked at me. "Janet, I know Pat was with you when you say Nita was dumped on your front step. But some guys here think you killed her earlier and then had one of your friends at the W.R.C. dump her on your doorstep, when Pat could give you an alibi. They say it's strange that Pat—a cop—was with you when the body was dumped, because everyone I talked to tells me you and Pat are through. So why is he with you—for the first time in a long time—the night you need an alibi?"

Me kill Nita? Could Larry really think that? "I loved Nita!" I said.

"Why would someone shoot Paul right in front of you?" Larry said. "Why wait until you got there to shoot him?"

"I don't know!" I cried. "Someone is trying to get me. I'm being followed. I'm getting hang-up calls. Someone put poison in Lech's food. You know Roach Roads threatened me."

"Are you trying to say someone shot Paul just to get you arrested?" Larry said, looking closely at me.

The starch went out of me. It sounded crazy the way Larry said it. "No," I said. "Of course not. Nobody would do that."

"I don't know," Larry said slowly. "The whole thing has a phony feel to it. It just doesn't hang right. You've got to tell me the truth, Janet. Are you sure Paul's shooting happened like you said? Are you sure you didn't see anyone there? Are you sure someone didn't tell you to go the bridge just at that time?"

I thought about Carmen. Carmen wanted me to go to the bridge. But she didn't give me the note as soon as I got to her house. She waited until I'd been there awhile. Could she have been waiting for a certain time before she handed it over?

No, that was crazy. Carmen didn't give me the note right away because her kids acting up put it right out of her mind. And Carmen couldn't have anything to do with my being a witness to Paul's murder. Carmen could not have sent me to the bridge so I would get in trouble. I would never believe that. Not even if she hated Paul because she thought he killed Nita. "No," I said, "nobody sent me to the bridge. I got the note and I went there because of the note."

"How could anyone know *when* you would get there?" Larry said. "The guys here think you are lying. They think there was no one there but you when Paul got shot."

"I didn't do it, Larry," I said. "I swear I didn't do it."

Larry turned off the tape recorder. "Go home, Janet. Get some rest. You look worn-out."

"You're not going to arrest me?" I said.

"Not at this time," he answered, his voice formal. "But please don't leave town."

"I never go anywhere," I said.

"And keep Lech with you," Larry told me, looking at me with an expression that made my heart turn over and my face feel hot.

"Always," I said.

*   *   *

Walking home, my steps dragged. Lech trotted close to me, his head turning from side to side. I could feel that he was tense. When I looked at him, I saw that the fur around his neck stood up and that his tail was stiff. The back of my neck felt prickly.

I was very tired. Maybe the reason I felt so weird was that I needed something to eat. We passed a deli and I went in and bought a carton of pasta salad and some cole slaw.

I came out and turned into an alley that was a shortcut home. I never took this route at night. But it was five o'clock and the sun was shining brightly, so I figured it would be okay. And I was so tired.

The alley was shady because the buildings cut off the sun's rays. One side was almost dark to my eyes after the brilliance of the sunlight. The garbage cans and dumpsters cast inky black shadows. Suddenly I heard a sound—a sound of a shot—and Lech let out a yelp.

I looked at him. Blood was gushing from his ear. "Lech!" I screamed. I flung myself over him as another shot rang out. I heard the sound of a siren. At the same time Pat came running down the alley.

"Janet! Janet! Are you okay?" He grabbed me, and as I was hanging on to Lech, he dragged both of us behind a dumpster, out of the line of fire.

"It's Lech!" I screamed. "They were shooting at him!

We've got to get him to a vet, quick! Oh, my God!"

Lech was making pathetic yelping sounds. I knelt over Lech, protecting him, while Pat stood in front of me, scanning the alleyway. "I heard two shots," he said. "There's a bullet hole in that wall behind where you were standing. Look, the shooter must have been over there." He pointed to a narrow walkway between two buildings.

"Yes," I said, gasping for breath. "I saw a flash there."

"I can't believe how stupid you are, walking alone down a dark alley!" He pulled out a gun and ran to the walkway. Standing against the wall, out of the line of fire, he pointed his gun toward the walkway. "Police!" he shouted. "Drop your weapons!"

"Forget that!" I screamed at him. "They're long gone. I heard them running away when the police sirens came this way. Where's your car? We have to get Lech to a vet!"

Pat stood there, peering down into the walkway, his gun pointed.

"Pat!" I yelled. "It's Lech! He's hurt bad. Come *on*!"

Pat turned and ran back to me. He pulled off his white T-shirt, ripped off a piece of it, and handed the piece to me. I balled it up and pressed it gently against Lech's ear. In an instant it was bright red.

Pat picked Lech up tenderly in his arms and ran down the alley, holding Lech. I followed. At the end of the alley we came out on the main street. A taxi was cruising by. We got in and Pat told the driver to take us to the animal hospital.

I looked down into Lech's brown eyes and saw his confusion and pain. "Don't worry, darling Lech," I murmured, "everything is going to be all right. You'll see. And I'll get the guy who did this to you, no matter what."

CHAPTER 9

First thing you need to know: Lech is okay. The bullet just grazed his ear. Although I have no proof, I'd bet anything that Lech dodged the bullet. He is such a smart dog, I wouldn't put it past him. Probably if he hadn't sensed the shooter in that walkway and moved, he would have been hit right in the belly and be dead now. I can hardly bear to think about it.

Lech seems a little blue, though. I think his pride was hurt. He is very proud of his guard-dog skills. We worked hard together so that he could learn them, and he takes his responsibilities seriously.

The day after the shooting in the alley, I decided I needed to go back to the bridge where Paul died. I checked in with Larry and told him I was going out of the city, that I needed a break. And I wanted to give Lech a special treat too.

When I told Larry this, there was a silence on the other end of the line.

"You don't have a car, do you?" Larry asked.

"No. But when I need one, I borrow an old clunker from a friend of Mrs. Gretzky," I said.

"Let me take you," Larry replied.

"Aren't you in the middle of a murder investigation?"

"That's okay," Larry said. He was too polite to say that I was the chief suspect, and he wanted to know what I was up to. "With everything that's been happening, I don't like to think about you going off alone. How about I come by and pick you up in half an hour?"

"Sure. See you then," I said. I hung up and went to the window and looked out. The sky was cloudless but seemed to be covered with a dull haze of heat. The air shimmered with light, but somehow it didn't feel like a bright sunny day. It was hot and there was no breeze.

The phone rang. I didn't answer it. It rang four times, and then the answering machine picked up. The tape Porsha had given me was in it. My voice said hello. Then suddenly the tape in the machine let out an ear-curdling, bloody scream—the most horrible, awful scream you ever heard. If I hadn't been expecting it, I am sure it would have made me jump through the roof.

Next came a loud horrible crash, then a bang like a shot. Then a high, shrill woman's voice started to laugh. It was an ugly sound, like a chalk scraping on a blackboard, and it sent shivers down my spine. The laugh sound slid down the scale, changing into a loud male roar. Next the voice on the tape chanted, "Beware, beware, beware," in an evil-sounding witchy voice. The sounds had all been blended like a piece of music, so that one slid into the next and the effect was bloodcurdling. Even though I had heard it before, it gave me the creeps. It ended with the usual beep.

My anonymous caller gasped in surprise, then blurted

out one swearword. His voice sounded kind of stunned. Then he hung up.

I hoped he had half the scare he'd been giving me. My W.R.C. friends and Larry now knew to call me on the cell phone, but I hadn't given the cell phone number to anyone else. Its number wasn't listed in my name so there was no way to find it. I no longer answered my regular phone, only my cell phone. That meant that the shrieks Porsha had put on my answering machine tape were my special present to my anonymous caller.

I thought about the voice I heard after the beep. The caller had been so surprised that he broke his usual silence and spoke that one swearword. A very familiar voice. A man's voice. If only he had said one or two more words, I might know for sure who it was. No such luck.

Of course I had tried having the calls traced. But the phone company reported back that they all came from different pay phones. Now at least I had learned something from the fact that the caller didn't know about my cell phone number.

A horn honked. I looked down into the street and saw Larry get out of his car and wave to me. Calling to Lech to come with, I headed out.

Larry, Lech, and I drove west on Dempster to the Edens Expressway. I told him I wanted to go north to where it was cool and green and there were trees.

"Did you have any special place in mind?" he asked me.

"I want to go back to the Bridge over Troubled Waters," I said. "Maybe I'll remember something more. And it is lovely there. Lech can run and explore a little."

"That's a good idea," Larry said. "I was going to ask you to do that. I need you to show me where you were standing and where the shot came from. I know you showed the cops who came when you called 911, but I need to see for myself. I've been putting off asking you because I thought going back there would be too hard on you."

"I know what you mean," I said. "But I can't stand not knowing what really happened."

Lech sat in the backseat of Larry's car. He looked kind of funny with a big bandage on one ear.

"What do you think about Lech's getting shot?" I asked Larry.

"It's kind of odd . . ." Larry began, then stopped.

"That Pat was right there," I finished for him.

"Yes."

"He's been 'right there' a lot, you know, " I said. "Just passing by when you and I were having dinner. Outside when we talked in the doughnut shop. Popping up when I went out to buy a pizza. Sitting across from my place in the little park the night Nita was killed."

"What do you think?" Larry asked.

"Maybe he's worried about me and trying to look after me," I said. But that is not what I thought. No matter what Pat said, I didn't think he cared about me. He was always telling me I was stupid and putting me down. His hanging around gave me a bad feeling.

"We got the bullets they shot at Lech," Larry said.

"Do they match the bullets that killed Nita and Paul?" I asked.

"Too soon to know," Larry said. "Maybe in a couple of days."

"If they do, would that mean I'd be off the hook for the murders?"

Larry sighed. "Not really. The guys who think you killed Paul think you had one of your friends helping you dump Nita's body. They think you had one of your friends fire wild shots at you in the alley to make us stop suspecting you."

"They think Lech was shot by accident?" I asked.

"Yeah."

"But that's not right!" I said.

"Didn't you say that as soon as Lech was shot, you protected him by covering him with your body, but someone shot again?"

"Yes, but it all happened in a few seconds. I pushed Lech out of the way and that second bullet just went by the place where he had been. Pat showed me the hole in the wall. It was low. Dog height, not person height."

"I know," Larry said. "I think you're right. Especially since you already told me about the poisoned burger the kids tried to give to Lech. I found those kids and talked to them. They said some man gave them the burger and paid them five bucks to give it to Lech. But they couldn't identify the man."

We drove in silence for a while. I was trying to put it all together: the attempts to kill Lech, Pat always being around, the hang-up calls, Roach's threats, Nita's and Paul's deaths. But I couldn't figure it out.

From time to time I turned to look at Lech. He was sitting up and gazing out the window and seemed to be enjoying himself. Despite the funny bandage on his ear, he looked like his old, alert, confident self.

When we arrived at the parking lot for the forest preserve, I opened the back door and Lech jumped out. He tilted his nose up and sniffed. Even I, with my human nose, could smell the sharp smell of growing things and the freshness of the air.

Larry, Lech, and I set off down the trail. The little stream ran alongside the trail, but it looked different today. When I had come before, it was fast-moving and brown, almost to the top of its banks.

Now it was clear and ran more slowly. In some places it looked shallower, and I could see gravel at the bottom.

The trail took a bend and in the distance we could see the bridge. I pointed it out to Larry.

"Is this where you stopped and Paul called out to you?" Larry asked.

"No," I said. "That's farther along."

We walked toward the bridge. "It's somewhere near here," I said. "I can't say the exact place. Go stand on the bridge—that might help."

Larry walked to the bridge and out onto the middle of it. I moved forward until, from where I stood, I could see him looking about the same as Paul had. The railing of the bridge was a bit below chest level on Larry, but Paul was shorter than Larry. "I was standing about here," I called to Larry.

Larry jogged back to me. He looked around. A small orange flag was attached to a spindly tree near where I stood. The police had put it there when I showed them where I stood the day I called 911.

"I'm going to walk for a while," I said. "I want to think."

"Okay," Larry said. "I'll scout around here and then catch up to you."

I headed off down the trail, Lech at my side.

To my right, the stream bubbled along.

Lech was having a great time. I had not given him the command to heel so he ran here and there, sniffing and peeing on things whenever he felt like it. Sometimes he would dart off into the trees but he always caught up to me again in a few minutes. I wished I could let him run free in the city like this.

We reached a place where the stream took a bend to the right. Just where it curved, a big willow leaned down over the water, casting dark shadows. The willow's long roots, twisted and old-looking, stuck up out of the stream bank and some went down into the water. One root looked almost like a bench, so I walked over to it and sat down on it. I took off my sandals and let my toes dangle into the water. It felt fresh and cool. I let my mind drift.

High above me, small clouds drifted over the blue sky. Shadows moved over the stream so that at times it sparkled in the sun and then that same place would look dark and mysterious.

The current came toward me from the direction of the bridge. Bits of wood floated downstream, and some were driven toward the willow where a few stuck between the roots.

I looked closer and saw that in some places, the old willow tree had quite a collection of junk caught among its tangled roots. Broken glass, grown thick from the movement of water, glittered like jewels. Bits of wood, polished by their time in the flowing water, glowed like lost treasures.

Then my eyes caught a glimmer of bright red. I looked closer. It was a piece of glass and something about it looked familiar. I leaned over and reached for it. That didn't work. I was wearing shorts, so I didn't need to worry about getting wet. I slid into the water and carefully lifted the red object out from the tangle of roots. I climbed back to my seat on the willow root and studied my find.

It was a large piece of clear glass with part of a label still stuck on it. The label was bright red. On the red label were the letters "CYN." The glass was thick, thicker than a beer bottle. I turned it over and over in my hand. "Look at this, Lech," I said.

Lech came over to me and I showed him the piece of glass. He sniffed at it. I could tell he saw nothing interesting about it. Probably it had no smell after being in the water.

I peered down into the place where the tangled roots had caught the piece of glass to see if there was anything else of interest there. Nothing caught my attention.

As I was staring down into the water, Larry came along the trail.

"Hey, Janet," he called. "What's up?"

"Larry," I said, "look what I found caught in the tree roots in the stream." I showed him the piece of glass.

He turned it over and over in his hand. "What do you think it is?" he asked.

"I think it's a part of a bottle of Cynar."

"Cynar?" Larry said. "What's that?"

"I know. I had never heard of it either," I said, "until Paul tried to make me drink some. It's an Italian drink he liked. I saw the bottle. It was heavy clear glass with a red label. A label just like this bit you can see stuck to the piece of glass."

"That's interesting," Larry said.

"I think you should look for the gun that shot Larry and Nita right here, down under these tree roots and also out in the stream near here," I said.

"You do, do you?" Larry said.

"Yes."

He sat down next to me. I could feel the heat from his body. Then he put his arms around me and murmured something in my ear. We began to kiss. He held me more tightly. It felt so wonderful I wanted that kiss to never end. But suddenly we both pulled back and looked at one another.

"This can't happen now," Larry said.

"I know," I said. "You have to do your job. I'm a murder suspect."

"Damn it all to hell," Larry said. "I know you didn't kill anybody."

"I didn't, I really didn't," I said softly. We were holding hands and I could feel the warmth of his trust and admiration. It flowed into my body through the touch of his fingers.

"But you're all mixed up in it, Janet," Larry said. "Nita being dumped on your doorstep. The attacks on Lech. Paul's killer waiting to kill him until you got here."

We talked around and around it, but I'm not sure either of us could really concentrate on the problem of murder. I was looking at Larry's clear blue eyes, the strong shape of his chin, the way his smile lit up his face. I was feeling the touch of his fingers. They transmitted joy through my whole body. I felt that something beautiful was beginning, and I feared that the terrible events I was caught up in might wreck it.

"You know I care about you," Larry said to me. "But until we wrap up this case, I can't do anything about it. If my boss knew, he'd take me off the case in a heartbeat. I don't want that to happen. If I stay on it, I can protect you."

"I won't say anything about how I feel to anybody, I promise," I said.

"And when other people are around, we have to act like just friends," Larry said. "That's really important."

"I'll try," I said. "I know you are my friend and that makes me very happy."

"I *am* your friend," Larry said, "and once we solve this, I want to be a lot more."

"We'd better solve it quick then," I said.

CHAPTER 10

The police found a gun in the stream, right near where I told Larry to search.

Larry came by that evening to tell me about it. He looked terrible. He hadn't shaved, his eyes were puffy, and his dress shirt had seen better days.

"I don't know how much longer I can protect you, Janet," Larry said. He sank down into the couch. I sat across from him, sipping on a Diet Coke. Lech lay across my feet, his head between his paws, his eyes on Larry.

"How come?" I asked. I wanted to comfort Larry; I could see how miserable he was. I longed to reach out to him. I tucked my hands underneath me so I wouldn't be tempted.

"Your story just doesn't hang together," Larry said.

"Which story?"

Larry smiled, but it was not a happy smile. "None of them do, actually. But the one about Paul's shooting is the real problem. You say you didn't see a shooter. But Paul was shot by a gun only a few inches from his head. Do you think, in the rain, Paul might have turned away from you to someone else on the bridge, someone you couldn't see? Someone whose body was hidden from you by Paul?"

I didn't see how that could be. I said, "Well, maybe." But my heart wasn't in it, and my doubt showed in my voice.

"Or maybe Paul was shot before you got there? You heard the shot before you came around the bend and when you got there, he was already dead?"

"No. It happened the way I said."

"There's got to be an explanation!" Larry said. "Your story can't be true. It doesn't fit the evidence. . . . Did you see Paul shoot himself and not want people to know? So you took the gun off the bridge and dropped it into the water downstream? I'd believe you if you told me that's what happened."

"No," I said. "That's not what happened."

"What does that leave, Janet?" Larry said. "*You* say Paul was alone and was shot on the bridge. That means he had to have been shot from a distance by someone in the trees. But he wasn't."

"Couldn't it have happened that way and then rain washed off the clues?"

"No. Rain or no rain, the wound itself proves he was shot from close up. He had the star-burst pattern on his face that only comes from being shot by a gun right next to the skin. Trust me, that's what happened. See how it looks? You were there and you say you didn't see anybody shoot Paul. But we know that's what had to have happened!"

Larry was telling me the evidence proved I was a liar. It was amazing that he still seemed to be giving me the benefit of the doubt. The clues piled up, all pointing toward me. I was starting to think maybe I was going crazy. Maybe my memory was playing tricks on me.

Larry looked at me as if expecting me to say something. When I didn't, he continued. "And now you go and find the gun. Do you know how that looks? Everyone except me is positive you knew where the gun was because you shot him and then you threw it into the water yourself. Like he had a gun, you and he struggled, and the gun went off."

I still didn't say anything. What was there to say? It seemed that what I saw with my own eyes couldn't have happened. "What about the gun?" I asked.

"That's another fact against you," Larry said. "The gun was a tomcat—that's a Beretta .32. A light little gun. Your gun was a .32 too, Janet."

My heart sank. "Was it my gun you found in the stream?"

"No way to know. The numbers were filed off. But it was the same caliber as yours. And here's something weird. The gun we found had a string tied to it."

"A string?" I asked, astonished. "Why would anyone tie a string to a gun?"

"Beats me. Someone had poked a string through the drilled hole in the thumb piece and tied it tightly. The string was about four feet long. Strong twine."

"I guess the gun couldn't have floated downstream? Paul shoots himself, drops the gun off the bridge, and then the current carries it to the willow tree?"

"Guns don't float," Larry said. "And we figure there's no way Paul could have shot himself and let the gun fall into the water. The bridge railing was too high. I tried it myself. Holding a gun to my head and then dropping it. Every time I tried it, the gun ended up on the bridge, not in the stream. I threw something that weighed about the same as that gun, fifteen ounces, in the water. It sank like a stone."

"Any clues on the piece of glass with the Cynar label?"

"It looks like it might be a broken piece of glass from a bottle of Cynar, all right. But so what? No fingerprints or anything like that."

"Did the gun you found in the stream shoot the bullets that they took out of Nita and Paul?"

"Too soon to be sure. But I have to tell you, Janet. As soon as the tests are done, if the murder bullets prove to be fired from the gun we found in the stream, I won't have any choice. I'm going to have to arrest you. I shouldn't even be giving you this information." He stared at me. "Are you sure there's not something you're not telling me?"

I looked back at him. Of course, there were a million things I wasn't telling him. Like that I was falling in love with him. Like that Carmen had given me the note Paul wrote inviting me to the bridge. Like whose voice I thought I had recognized when I heard the swear word on my tape, the voice of the hang-up caller. "I feel like I'm in a bad dream," I said softly.

Larry looked at me. "Know what I think? I think someone's out to get you. I don't know how they did this. I don't know how they shot Paul and made it look like you did it. But I have a cop's hunch about this. The guys at the station, they've seen my hunches prove out before. So they've let me run with this but not for much longer."

"Do you think it could be Roach?" I asked. "He threatened me."

"I'd like it to be him," Larry said. "But there is no proof. And if he did it, I can't figure out how. And something else: I can see Roach doing a lot of bad things. But killing Paul and Nita and framing you for it? I don't know. It seems way too risky and complicated. He's had people killed. If that's what he wants to do with you, why doesn't he just do it?"

I looked down at Lech. I figured with Lech to protect me, I must be kind of hard to kill.

Larry jumped up. "I better go now. Please think about what I said. There must be *something* you saw, something you're not telling me. If you don't come up with a better story . . . "

He looked at me. His eyes looked incredibly sad. "See you," he said. Then he was gone.

I walked over to the window and looked out. Larry came out of the front door. His head was down and his hands were in his pockets. He looked miserable. He headed off down the street.

My cell phone rang. I answered.

"Janet?" It was Sally, but I hardly recognized her voice. She sounded so strange. "Are you at home? I need to talk to you."

"Sure, come over. Better do it quick," I said. "I may not be here much longer. Larry says they're going to arrest me if the gun they found in the stream is the one that shot Paul and Nita. And I'm sure it is."

Normally, if I said something like that, Sally would have screamed, "Oh, my God!" But this time, all she said was, "I'm on my way. I'll be there in ten minutes." Then she hung up.

If ever there was a time for a cigarette, this was it. I started frantically looking around. Could I have maybe hidden some in my bedroom? Maybe in the chest of drawers under my T-shirts?

No.

Under my jeans?

No.

What about on the closet shelf?

I dragged a kitchen chair into the bedroom and climbed up to look there. Dust bunnies. A broken lamp.

Some mending that had been waiting for attention for years. No cigarettes.

Face it, Janet. You are in serious shit. Even a man who cares about you thinks you killed Paul Moro.

I climbed down off the chair. Lech was looking at me curiously. Maybe he thought I might have hidden dog biscuits on the closet shelf. "Nothing up there but junk, Lech," I said. Of course, I knew that. I'd already looked for my gun up there when Larry asked about it. "Maybe nothing up *here* but junk," I told my dog, pointing to my head. Why couldn't I figure out what had happened to Paul? I had been right there, for heaven's sake! I had seen him shot with my own eyes. If he was shot by someone standing right next to him, I had to have seen it.

But my memory wouldn't show me the right picture. When I thought back, all I saw was the rain pouring down, the blurred shape of Paul. Then the shot. Then Paul falling below the bridge railing and disappearing from view. Now I knew from what Larry had said *that couldn't have happened*.

I heard Sally buzz the downstairs doorbell, and I went down to let her in. She rushed past me into my apartment. "Where's Lech?"

Lech was standing right there. Sally threw herself on him, hugging him and kissing him. "Oh, my God, you poor thing," she said. "Look at that bandage on your ear. Does it hurt? They tried to kill you, darling doggie! Oh, my God, I can't believe it."

Sally had not seen Lech since he had been shot, but still I thought she was overdoing it.

"He's okay," I said. "How about saying hi to me too?"

Sally sat down on the sofa. I saw that her face was very white. She had dark circles under her eyes. "I have to tell you, Janet," she said.

I sat down across from her. "Tell me what?"

"I don't know why I love him, but I can't help it!" Sally wailed.

"What?" I said again.

Sally leaned forward. "It's about Roach Roads and Baxter," she whispered.

"What about them?"

"I found out Baxter is back working for Roach," Sally said. "I know I should have told you. I didn't want to believe it. I asked him about it and he lied and so I kidded myself. I thought he'd changed, Janet, you have to believe me!" She stretched out her arm and touched my hand.

"I believe you," I said.

"Baxter bought me a diamond ring and took me nice places. He took me shopping and said I could buy whatever I wanted. He bought me French perfume."

"Oh, Sally," I said.

"I pretended everything was okay," Sally said. "Then this morning I went to work at Hair-Today. I was almost there when I remembered I had forgotten my new ring." Sally had a tear in her eye. "I wanted to show it off to the girls at the shop, so I went back for it. When I had left, Baxter was sleeping, so when I went back, I opened the apartment door real quiet. I didn't want to wake him, you know?"

I nodded.

"As soon as I opened the door, I heard men's voices in the kitchen. I recognized Roach's voice right away. You know how it sounds like a machine?" Sally wiped her eyes.

"I remember his voice," I said.

"I was scared. I hate that voice of his," Sally said. "It gives me the creeps. So real quiet, I tiptoed into the bedroom to get my ring. Then I heard it."

"Heard what?" I asked.

"Your name. They were talking about you," Sally whispered. Now tears were running down her cheeks.

"What did they say?" I whispered back.

"Roach said, 'Janet Barkin is making a fool of us. This can't go on. Next thing, she'll have that cop, Larry Keegan, believing we aced Paul and Nita. She's got Keegan wound around her finger. He helped her before. We have to get her. Didn't I tell you to take out her dog? Once we get the dog, she's ours.'

"And Baxter said, 'Don't worry. The dog is dead. Count on it.'

"And Roach said, 'That's what you told me yesterday, but you shot at the dog and you missed, right?'"

"Oh, Sally," I said, "Baxter shot Lech." I had always hated Baxter. But how I had felt before was nothing compared to how I felt now. If Baxter had been in front of me, I would have jumped on him and torn his eyes out. Or tried to, anyway. I could feel my heart pounding and a noise like roaring in my ears.

Sally continued. "Then Baxter said, 'It's like the devil is in that dog. He sticks to Barkin like glue. I had him dead to rights. Then at the last minute he must have smelled me or something, because he moved and my first shot just winged him. Janet pulled him away from my second. Then out of nowhere, there's that cop, Janet's ex-husband, Pat Barkin? He turns up. So I had to get out of there. No time to try again.'"

Sally wiped her eyes again, smearing her mascara into dark smudges under her eyes. She leaned closer to me and took both my hands in hers. "Janet, I knew I had to hear more. So real quiet, I tippy-toed into the living room and stood by the door to the kitchen. I looked in. Baxter and Roach were drinking coffee. They had a cardboard box on the table. I heard what they said. They are going to kill you, Janet. You and Lech both. I heard their plan. I had to tell you."

Sally put her face into her hands and began to sob. Through her sobs, she said, "I know you have to tell Larry. He'll catch them both and this time Baxter will go to jail for a long time. And he'll know it was me who told on him. He'll hate me and I'll never see him again. Oh, Janet, I wish I didn't love him. I know he doesn't mean to be bad. On the outside he's tough and angry, but deep inside he isn't bad. Truly he isn't. Deep down in him, there's this sad, hurt little boy. But what can I do? I can't let him kill my best friend! Oh, my God. . . ."

I got up and went to Sally and put my arms around her. She leaned on my shoulder and sobbed her heart out. In between her sobs she told me what was in the cardboard box and what Roach and Baxter had planned for Lech and for me. Her whole body was shaking. I patted her back and from time to time, I said, "That's okay . . . it will be all right . . . everything will work out."

But of course, it would not be okay. I would call Larry and he would come over. Sally would tell him the plan she had heard Baxter and Roach cook up in her kitchen. She would tell him what was in the cardboard box. If all went well, everything Sally dreaded would happen. Roach and Baxter would be arrested. Baxter would go to jail for a long time. Sally would lose him forever.

And that was the good news.

The bad news was, if the plan to catch them in the act failed, they might succeed in killing Lech and me. If not, they would try again. Either way, Lech and I would be dead.

CHAPTER 11

We had agreed that I should stay in my apartment all the next day until evening—when we were putting our plan into action. Porsha would take Lech for his morning walk, so I had a lot of time to kill. I spent part of that day—a day that seemed to last forever— going over everything that had happened in my mind. When that didn't get me anywhere, I explained it to Lech. Talking out loud to Lech helps me see things more clearly.

"Sally didn't want to help," I told Lech. "You understand that, don't you?"

I was sitting in the living room. The TV was on but neither Lech nor I watched it. Early Sunday evening there's nothing worth watching anyway. No cartoons for Lech.

"When Larry asked Sally to help catch Baxter and Roach, she just sat there looking at the floor. I felt bad. I bet you did too," I said to Lech. "We put her in a real bind."

Lech lifted his head and gazed at me, waiting to see what I would say next.

"Who could blame her?" I asked Lech.

Lech thumped his tail on the floor. He agreed with me that asking for Sally's help in trapping Baxter was asking a lot.

I could still see Sally's face. After her confession to me, I had called Larry on his cell phone. He had come right over. He had asked Sally a lot of questions. His voice was kind, but I don't know how much that helped. I could see Sally was being ripped apart, torn between her loyalty to me, her oldest friend, and her love for Baxter. She had just sat there answering Larry, without looking at either of us, and it seemed like she got smaller and smaller each time she spoke.

"There's one thing I don't get," Larry had said to Sally. "How do they intend to get Janet to go into the park late at night?"

Sally swallowed. "Baxter promised Roach he'd make me help him. Baxter said that I would do whatever he told me to. He told Roach he'd make me call Janet and ask her to meet me in the park."

"Has Baxter asked you to do that yet?" Larry asked.

"Yes," Sally said, still not looking at me.

"And what did you say," Larry asked gently. "Did you agree to do it?"

"I said yes," Sally replied in a very soft voice, so soft I could barely hear her. "But then as soon as Baxter went out, I called Janet and came over here to tell her everything."

"You did the right thing," Larry said. "You just keep on doing everything Baxter tells you to. As long as we know their plans, we can deal with them."

"Lech will protect me," I said.

"But—" Sally began.

"Lech would never fall for their dumb trick," I said. "Don't worry about it."

"He has to fall for it," Larry said. "Or we can't catch Roach and Baxter in the act. Roach has a top lawyer. That lawyer has already got the judge to agree to hear Roach's appeal on the other murder charge. And Roach got bail. We won't get him for this attempted murder just on Sally's say-so. He and Baxter actually have to carry out at least a part of their plan. We have to catch them in the act."

That was last night. Last night, with Larry sitting there, I felt brave and sure I could handle everything. But that was then.

And this was now. Soon it would get dark. Then Sally would call. Then it would all happen.

I looked at Lech. "You're going to hate it, Lech," I said to him. "But it's the only way to get them. Larry thinks so and I trust Larry."

Lech tilted his head. I could see he wasn't so sure he trusted Larry. He thought Larry meant well, but too much could go wrong with the plan.

I knelt down beside Lech and petted him. The fur on his back felt smooth and soft and warm. He twisted his head around and licked my knee. I leaned over and hugged him. "You have to be brave, Lech," I whispered.

But of course, Lech knew what I really meant. He was brave already. The person who needed to be brave was me.

The phone rang. My heart started to bang against my ribs. I picked up the receiver.

"Hi, Janet." It was Sally. Her voice sounded tense and fake.

"Hi, Sally, how's it going? Is Baxter there, listening?"

"Yes, me too," Sally said. "Sunday is such a dead night. Baxter's gone out and I have nothing to do. How about going out and having a coffee, go to a flick, or something?"

"I'm cool," I said.

"How about you meet me at the park across from your house, say around nine-thirty? Wait under the big tree. I've got Baxter's car, so you can bring Lech. He won't mind waiting in the car while we're at the movie. I'll drive by and you can hop right in. Okay?"

"I got it," I said. Of course, Sally knew I'd never leave Lech locked in a car while I went to a movie. But obviously this dumb invitation was Baxter's idea. It was so dumb—me waiting in the park after dark—that I would have wondered what was the matter with Sally if I didn't already know.

"See you in the park then," Sally said. "Don't forget to bring Lech to protect you."

"Right," I said. I banged down the phone. I looked at Lech. "I hate this," I said.

Lech banged his tail on the floor twice. I could see he hated it too.

*   *   *

Standing at my window, a bag of nacho chips in my hand, I ate and watched the daylight quickly fade into night. The streetlights came on and fewer and fewer people were walking by. Sunday is a quiet evening. The park across the street was poorly lit, and it seemed to get dark there faster than anywhere else. The tree in the center looked like a cloud of blackness. Its branches cast inky shadows so that underneath there seemed to be a dark hole. Only an idiot would stand there. Soon I would be that idiot.

I kept looking for the police, but I didn't see anybody. They were probably in one of the vans parked on the street, but how could I tell for sure?

The lights were off in my living room, so anyone looking up at my window couldn't see me.

I kept my eye on the tree. Surely I would see Baxter

approaching it. But I didn't.

I stuck my hand into the bag of chips and all that came up were a few greasy crumbs. I had eaten the whole bag. I looked at my watch. It was five minutes after nine. Time to go.

I called to Lech. "I am so sorry, Lech," I said. I felt tears in my eyes. "You are going to hate this. Be brave. Now, heel!"

Down the steps we went. Across the street, with Lech trotting just behind my left leg as he had been taught.

Walking across the faintly lit park toward that tree was one of the hardest things I ever did. Everyone had promised me that Lech would be okay. But I kept wondering, what if something goes wrong?

Halfway to the tree, Lech stopped. His ears went up. His tail went stiff. He stared at the tree. The fur around his neck rose up. Then all his fur rose up so he looked twice as big. He growled deep in his throat.

"Come on, Lech," I said in a fakey-cheerful voice. "What's the matter? We promised Sally we'd wait under the tree."

What a dumb plan Baxter and Roach had cooked up. I would never have gone near that tree with Lech acting this way, if it wasn't part of my deal with Larry.

I took a step forward. Lech nudged me with his nose. As clearly as if he had spoken, I heard him say, "Danger, don't go there."

"I'm sorry, Lech," I whispered. I leaned down and patted him on the head. "We have to do this."

I moved forward. Lech did not. He barked loudly.

"Lech!" I commanded. "Heel!"

Still he didn't move. Instead he gave a loud, high yelp, a warning that sent a chill up my spine.

"Lech!" I said in my strongest voice. "I mean it. Heel! Now!"

Lech was trained to obey. We had spent hundreds, maybe thousands of hours working together. Lech knew that particular command voice and he knew his duty. His head dropped, his tail went between his legs, and he came along behind me. He was so tense and wary he was quivering. Little moaning noises came out of him as I walked under the tree.

Suddenly he butted me with his head. At the same instant, a big net fell from the tree on top of Lech. Lech was snarling, barking, struggling in the net. Baxter dropped from the branches above and sprayed something into the net. The snarling and barking stopped.

As soon as the net dropped, I opened my mouth to scream. But a gloved hand pressed over my mouth, while a strong arm wrapped itself around me so hard it felt as if my bones would crunch together. Roach Roads's voice hissed into my ear. "You don't want your dog killed? Then shut up and don't move. Act normal."

Baxter leaned over the bundle of net and began wrapping a rope around it.

"The dog is just out long enough for us to take you," Roach hissed. "If you do what I say, we won't hurt your stupid dog."

Where were the cops? Where was Larry? Roach began to pull me toward a car that I now saw had parked in front of the park. It was Roach's big, dark green Jaguar.

Baxter was dragging the net with Lech. As we came out of the shadow of the tree I saw that Lech was not moving inside the thick netting. When Sally explained to Larry the chemical that Roach planned to spray on Lech to make him be quiet, Larry had checked on it and then told me Lech would be okay in a few minutes. But something must have gone wrong. Lech was so still!

I couldn't wait anymore. I had to protect Lech. Once

they had us both in the car, who knew what they might do to him? I had to free him and get him to a vet!

I went limp.

"What the—" Roach hissed. "Get up! If I have to drag you, someone might notice something's going down. If that happens, your dog is dead meat." He yanked at me, trying to get me to stand on my legs, which I had let go soft as spaghetti.

Then I straightened my legs. With all my strength I kicked out, hooking one of his legs so that he lost his balance.

We both fell down, Roach on top of me.

Roach shouted, "Baxter! Forget the mutt! Get over here!"

I struggled harder.

Roach's hand slipped off my mouth.

I opened my mouth and shouted at the top of my lungs, "Help! Help!"

I felt Roach's hands around my neck. I kicked out. I twisted. I had to get away. Baxter had Lech! Roach's hands tightened like a band of iron closing around my neck.

Beyond Roach's head, I saw the streetlight go dim, slide across the dark sky, then go out.

*   *   *

The next thing I knew, a strange face was leaning over me and beyond it, I could see flashing red lights. In the distance I heard loud swearing. Baxter's voice.

Then I heard a familiar yelp, and a soft, black furry nose pressed up against my cheek.

Lech! I tried to speak but no words came out.

I was lying on my back on a stretcher in the park. Larry's voice said something and the strange man stepped away and Lech was there, licking my face. I threw my arms around him.

Then Larry stood beside Lech.

"It's okay, Janet," Larry said. "Lech is fine, you're going to be fine, and we have Baxter and Roach in custody."

I started to sit up, but Larry pressed me gently back down upon the stretcher. "The paramedics want you to rest a minute. Roach tried to strangle you and you passed out. We need to take you to the emergency room and have you checked out. I'm just going to run Lech over to Mrs. Gretzky's first. But he won't leave you without your permission."

How I loved Larry at that moment. With everything going down, he wanted to be sure Lech was okay. "Go on, go with Larry," I said to Lech. My voice came out in a croak. "Go." I pointed to Larry.

Lech moved away from me. He stood by Larry's side, and they crossed the street to our place. A moment later, Larry was back.

"How long have I been out?" I said, struggling to sit up again. The paramedic gently settled me back on the stretcher. He and another picked it up and began walking me toward the waiting ambulance. Larry walked alongside.

"Not long," Larry said. "The same for Lech. Their chemical spray stunned him long enough for them to get him tied up. As soon as we untied him, got the net off, and splashed a little water on him, he seemed fine. A little confused at first, but fine now."

"Did Baxter or Roach say anything about Paul and Nita?" I asked.

We reached the ambulance. They slid me inside. Larry leaned in.

"I'll talk to you later. Sorry you had to go through this.

We wanted to catch them in the act, but our timing stunk." Larry sounded angry for a moment. "I'm really sorry, Janet," he said. "I never meant for Roach to get his hands on you. But I have to say, it was great how you fought him off. You are one brave woman."

"Are you sure Lech is okay?" I asked anxiously. "Are you sure the stuff they used to stun him didn't cause any damage? Maybe he ought to go to the vet—"

"He's fine, Janet," Larry said.

The doors to the ambulance closed.

I sank back on the stretcher, sick at heart. It looked like we had Baxter and Roach out of commission. But we still didn't know who had killed Paul and Nita, or why.

We still didn't know who had been making the anonymous hang-up calls.

We still didn't know who had been following me everywhere.

We still didn't know what would happen next.

And I could see, in my mind's eye, Roach's angry black eyes glaring at me. I could feel—as if it were happening this very minute—his cold hands tightening around my neck, choking the life out of me.

CHAPTER 12

"So let's this get straight," Porsha said. "Like, what exactly did Roach and Baxter think they were doing?"

We were all sitting around my place: Lech, Mrs. Gretzky, Sally, Porsha, and me. Mrs. Gretzky had brought some coffee cake. The warm cake filled my apartment with the smell of cinnamon. Porsha's mama had made a big pot of hot tea with lemon and honey and sent it up with Porsha. She had told Porsha to tell me that the honey would soothe my throat.

I lay on the couch with Lech on the floor beside me. My neck ached. There were big bruises where Roach's fingers had pressed against it, and it hurt to swallow.

I had spent the night after the adventure in the park lying awake, thinking. Reliving the moment when the net fell on Lech. Also dreading the day when Larry would have to arrest me. It was only a matter of time now. Maybe because I had helped the cops get Baxter and Roach, they would be nice and give me a day or two to recover from getting strangled.

But it would only be the calm before the storm. I had seen it in Larry's eyes when he brought me back from the hospital last night.

"Janet?" Porsha's voice cut into my thoughts and I snapped back into the present. Back to my apartment with the early morning light filling the living room, the smell of hot coffee cake and cinnamon, and my friends gathered around. All waiting for me to tell the story of what had happened in the park the night before.

"Okay," I said. My voice was soft, so everybody leaned forward as I spoke.

"Here's what happened," I said. "Sally overheard Roach and Baxter plotting to kill me. She heard them make their plan to put Lech out of action and then snatch me."

Lech, hearing his name, pricked up his ears and looked at me. I smiled at him.

"Sally saw a cardboard box on her kitchen table. Listening to them talk, she found out that they had a big net and some stuff they could spray on Lech to knock him out. They had tried to shoot Lech and that hadn't worked. So they planned to drop a big, tough net on him from the tree. Then when he couldn't move, they would knock him out, tie him up, take him somewhere, and . . ."

I took a deep breath. Then I went on. "Once Lech was out of the way, they could kill me. Their plan was to get me in the car, then take me somewhere out of town and shoot me. They would do it from close up and leave the gun there—try to make it look like suicide."

"I thought they wanted to torture you to make you suffer," Porsha said.

"They didn't have the time for that anymore," Sally said. "The way it looked to them, Janet had made Roach look like a fool. Roach felt that no one would take him seriously as long as they knew Janet had got him arrested, had ratted on him, and was still out and around."

"So it was Roach and Baxter who tried to poison Lech with the burger?" Porsha asked.

"Yes," I said. "They knew they couldn't get me as long as Lech protected me. First they tried to poison him. But that didn't work. Then they tried to shoot him. That didn't work either. So they came up with this net plan. But Sally overheard and because of her, they didn't get away with it." I looked at Sally. She tried to smile, but she looked miserable. She had done the right thing, but it had brought her no happiness.

I continued my explanation. "So some of the stuff that has been going on we can now put onto Roach and Baxter. But—the problem is—not all of it. I don't think Roach and Baxter are the ones who have been following me and making hang-up calls to my home phone number. How would they get an unlisted number? And I don't think Roach and Baxter killed Nita and Paul either."

"Those two guys are no-good bums," Mrs. Gretzky said. "Why don't you think they were the ones who killed Paul and Nita?"

"Why should they? What would it get them?" I replied. "Paul was paying Roach protection. Nita was nothing to Roach. They had no reason to harm either of them."

"You got any ideas, Janet?" Mrs. Gretzky asked.

"About who is following me and making the hang-up calls, yes," I said. "Porsha, you know that scary tape you made for my answering machine? It startled the hang-up caller so much he said something. I heard his voice. I think I recognized it."

"Who was it?" Sally asked.

My throat hurt. All this talking was tiring me out. "I can't talk about it yet," I said.

Porsha jumped up. "I got to get to school," she said. She looked at Sally. "You going to the W.R.C. office today?"

"Yes," Sally said. "It's Monday. Hair-Today is closed on Mondays so I always work a full day at the W.R.C. on Mondays."

"We got to get down and think hard," Porsha said. "We have to find out who killed Paul and Nita, and how. We can't just wait for the cops to arrest Janet. Look, I have to get to school now. But let's all meet at the office after school and brainstorm."

"You think we can figure it out when the police can't?" Sally asked. Her voice was flat. She looked so sad, my heart went out to her.

"Yeah, I do," Porsha said. "The difference between them and us is that we *know* Janet had nothing to do with it. See you later." She jumped up, grabbed her backpack, and rushed off.

A few minutes later, Sally and Mrs. Gretzky left too. I looked at my watch. It was eight-fifteen. I figured I'd better take Lech out for his morning walk. I got up slowly from the couch.

Down the stairs we went. I walked slowly. Every bone in my body hurt. I had big dark bruises on my thighs, my arms, and my shoulders. The skin on my knees was bandaged, since I had scraped them falling. The hospital had taped my ribs too. I guess I had fought Roach harder than I remembered.

On the street it was already very warm, but it was clouding over. Off to the east I could see dark clouds moving over the sky, and the wind was rising.

Lech and I crossed to the park. Lech seemed to have no bad memories of the place. He peed in his usual places, and we did our morning poop-and-scoop. Then we walked along the street. The tea had been good but I felt like a coffee. I walked slowly in the direction of a coffee shop I liked.

Suddenly I felt the skin on the back of my neck prickle. This time, I whirled around. We were passing a sidewalk that went between two buildings to the alleyway behind. Lech was staring into it. I ran as fast as I could down the sidewalk.

I heard footsteps running ahead of me.

I came out into the alley. I saw a man running away.

"Get him!" I told Lech, pointing at the man.

Lech took off down the alley after the man. They turned a corner and disappeared from view.

A few minutes later, I caught up to them. The man stood there with Lech pinning him up against the back of a building, growling low in his throat. The man was Pat.

"Hi, Janet," Pat said with a big charming smile. "Call off the dog, will you? What's his problem anyway? This is stupid, letting your dog chase people down alleys. What's the matter with you?"

"It's okay, Lech," I said.

Lech gave his head a little shake and then trotted over to me.

"No." I said. "The question is, what's *your* problem?"

As we spoke, I started walking back to the street. I didn't want to talk to Pat, standing in a dark, smelly alley. Back on the street we walked along without speaking until we came to a coffee shop. I think we both knew it was time to talk. Really talk.

Telling Lech to stand guard outside, I opened the door to

the coffee shop and went in. Pat followed. We both ordered coffee at the counter and then chose a table and sat down.

"Pat," I said. "I know it's you who's been stalking me."

"Say what?" Pat said. He looked really surprised. "Stalking you? What are you talking about?"

"I recognized your voice the first time that crazy tape was in my answering machine."

Pat's expression changed. "Okay, I have been calling you and hanging up. I wanted to know if you were home. I wanted to hear your voice, I don't know . . . but stalking you? Come on!"

"Why are you always around, Pat?" I asked him.

"You were glad to see me when they shot at Lech," Pat said. His face was red and his big smile was gone. I could see he was getting angry. "You sure needed me then. And where was your Larry Keegan when Roach Roads tried to strangle you? If it'd been me, I would never have let that happen. You're so crazy, someone's got to protect you."

Now I was getting mad. "So who nominated you? What gives you the right? I can protect myself!"

"I saw you kissing him!" Pat said. "He can't have you. You're my wife! Forever! Mine."

"Are you saying you love me?" I asked him.

"Well, of course I love you! How stupid can you be? Haven't I been following you everywhere to be sure you're safe? You need me, Janet. You can't make it on your own."

I suddenly felt very tired. I knew that Pat believed what he said. He thought he loved me. He thought stalking me was the same as protecting me. He thought scaring me half to death with weird hang-up calls was okay. He thought keeping me away from Larry Keegan was his right and duty. He didn't like me. He didn't respect me. He didn't want me to take the chances that grown-ups have to take if they want to be brave and do things. He didn't want me to get hurt, which has to happen sometimes to people—even people you love. Pat reminded me of Paul Moro, though I was sure he wasn't nearly so crazy. But there was something similar in their ideas about love.

"If you love someone, you don't tell them they are stupid every time you open your mouth," I said.

Pat looked down at his hands. "I'm just trying to take care of you, don't you understand?" he said. "I can't let you go. I'm afraid something is going to happen to you. Ever since you started with this W.R.C. thing, I've been going crazy inside, worrying about you. I feel like I need to watch you to be sure you are okay."

I didn't say anything. I didn't know what to say.

"I know you love me too," Pat said.

I looked at him. "I do and I don't," I said. I remembered the box of pictures I still hadn't thrown out. "We were married and I gave you all the love I had to give. But you hurt me too much, Pat. The drinking. The other women. The lies. The broken promises. So the love I feel for you is kind of a sad thing. More like a memory of something. I could never be happy with you. And you weren't happy with me. You were never proud of me. You thought of me as a stupid, fat loser, and in your heart you still do. It's just no good between us. There's no respect."

Pat stared at me. I saw that he didn't understand anything I had said. "Respect? What are you talking about? You don't fool me. It's Larry Keegan, isn't it?" Pat pointed a finger at me. "It's because he's a lieutenant and makes more money and everything."

"Okay, don't understand," I said. Why couldn't I make Pat understand? What was his problem? Was it because he just couldn't face it, that a woman wouldn't want him? Was it that being dumped hurt his feelings too much? "But now that I'm sure it was you," I said, "I won't let you keep doing this. It's going to stop, or you are going to be in big trouble."

"Oh yeah? How could *you* get me into big trouble? You plan to write me letters and put up posters like you did with Paul? A lot of good that did."

"Pat, you don't get it. You've been stalking me. If I report it to the captain at the precinct, you could be suspended. If I tell the newspaper how an undercover cop stalks and harasses his wife, they'll believe me. After all, I'm the one who was on TV for getting Roach, and I just did it again last night."

Pat went pale.

"The police won't want it in the papers that one of theirs is stalking and harassing his wife. I even have your voice on my machine. On an unlisted number. Who else do I know who can get unlisted numbers but a cop? And it's against the rules to do that for your private life."

Pat wasn't thinking straight, or he would have realized that one swearword on an answering machine tape wouldn't amount to anything. Because now I could see from his face, I had him.

"See what I mean?" I said. "Do we have a deal? You let me lead my life without your so-called protection and your so-called love, and I don't report you to the captain."

"But I can't let Larry Keegan win!" Pat blurted out.

I stood up. When I did, I could feel my ribs ache and the torn skin sting as it stretched over my knees. What a joke, my telling Pat I could protect myself. Protect myself? I could barely walk.

"Larry Keegan has nothing to do with you and me," I said. "Face it, Pat. I don't love you the way you want. I don't want you in my life. I know what you've been doing and if you don't stop it, your boss is going to know too."

I looked down at him. "So, do we have a deal?" I asked.

Pat didn't answer.

"Pat?" I said.

"Okay, okay, shut up, shut up!"

"Pat? *Do we have a deal?*"

"I said okay," Pat spat out. "You got your deal. I won't follow you and watch out for you and check up on you on the phone. But don't blame me when Larry Keegan arrests you for murder. You'll be all on your own then!"

CHAPTER
13

That afternoon, we gathered around in the W.R.C. office. I think we all knew that if we couldn't solve the Paul-and-Nita murders, it would be the end for the W.R.C. I would be arrested and the W.R.C. would be totally discredited.

I had bought a box of doughnuts and the box was open on the desk. We pulled up our chairs. Outside, there was the occasional crack of thunder and huge towering thunderclouds raced across the sky. As we spoke, the storm broke and the rain came pouring down.

"The police have tried to figure out what really happened when Paul was killed," I said. "They are sure I am lying about what I saw. But I'm not."

"We all know that," Sally said. Everyone nodded their agreement.

"But the problem is, no one can figure out what really happened, how Paul was shot," I said. "So let's forget about that for a moment. Let's try to solve it another way. I think we need to figure out who wanted Paul and Nita dead. If we can understand *why* they were killed, maybe the *how* will be easier to figure out."

Mrs. Gretzky leaned back in her chair. I could see that her legs were swollen, and I knew she must be feeling uncomfortable. But she wanted to help. "When you're an old lady like me, some things—you just know them. And this thing—it seems like Paul couldn't take it that the lady he loved told him no, I don't want you. It seems that he couldn't hear it. He couldn't stand it. Some men, when they get angry, when they can't have what they want, they go crazy. From what you say, Janet, I think Paul—he got crazy. So then he killed Nita."

Sally said, "I agree with you. I think Paul was crazy too. But no matter how crazy, he loved Nita. Why would he kill her? And even if he did, then who killed him?"

Porsha said, "Sally has a point. Why would Paul kill Nita? He loved her. Sure, I can see Paul wanting to kill you, Janet. He was mad enough. He blamed you for all the letters and at the end there, I think he blamed you for Nita not wanting him. If you had told me it was him who poisoned Lech or him who was stalking you, I would have believed that. But you say it was Roach who went after Lech and it was Pat who was doing the stalking?"

"Yeah. This whole thing has been so hard to figure out, because all our enemies were after us and it was tricky to tell who was doing what. But now we know it was Roach and Baxter who tried to kill Lech and me. And it was Pat who was doing the stalking and hang-up calls." I sighed. "I think we've put a stop to them. But you know, Porsha, I think you said something important. Whoever killed Paul and Nita wanted me to be blamed. And if it wasn't Roach and it wasn't Pat, then that leaves . . . Paul."

"But how would Paul know you would go to Carmen's and get the note? Because it was that note in your purse that really dumped you into it," Porsha said.

"He knew I would pay a condolence call on Carmen. So first he kills Nita. Then he goes to see Carmen. She tells him that I will come by that afternoon. He leaves a note getting me to go to the bridge. Then he goes there with his bottle of Cynar. He drinks it to give himself courage. He waits until I show up. Then he shoots himself and I get blamed."

"But that makes no sense!" Porsha said. She got up and began to dance a little hip-hop dance of frustration. "No sense at all! If it was Paul who framed you, and, let's say, Paul who killed Nita, that can't be right. Because the same gun killed Nita that killed Paul. And we know Paul didn't kill himself! This is driving me crazy!"

Porsha's words caused the beginnings of an idea to take shape my mind. I struggled to get it to come into focus. "I think you've got something there!" I said excitedly. "Now listen, let's say it's Paul. He thinks—him and Nita—they're Romeo and Juliet. If he can't have her, no one will. Their great love has to end in death."

Sally said, "It's so sad. You read about it happening. A man shoots his ex and then himself. I don't get it. I'll never get it."

But I hardly heard her. I went on thinking out loud. "But before he dies, Paul wants to get revenge on me. Because he's decided it's all my fault that he can't get Nita back. It's the W.R.C. that's to blame, and he figures I told Nita to stand up to him. So he makes his plans. He kills Nita. Then he gets me to the bridge. He keeps that note from me in his pocket and sends me a note from him asking me to meet him there. He knows that note will get me in trouble with the cops. He puts a map on the note so I will keep it with me. After all, he could have just asked Carmen to tell me how to get to the bridge. She knew. But no, he draws a map. And me, like a dope, I do just what he wants. I take the note and go to the bridge."

"The gun—" Porsha began.

But I was on a roll. "That's why he filed the numbers off his gun!" I said. "So no one will be able to prove it was his. And they'll think maybe it was mine."

"That's great," Mrs. Gretzky says. "This story you're telling, it sounds true. It's how a man crazy with love can be."

"But Janet," Porsha said, "you're forgetting. You were there. You didn't see Paul shoot himself. You heard a shot and you didn't see him kill himself."

I was really excited now. "Of course I didn't. It was raining and it was hard to see clearly. He called my name to be sure it was me; then he turned his back. I was too far to see exactly what happened. He planned it like that! Who else could? Who else would?"

Porsha stopped her dancing and came back and sat down. "This is all cool," she said. "But if Paul shot himself, how did the gun get in the stream, far away from the bridge?"

*   *   *

It was pouring rain late that afternoon. It gave me a weird feeling to realize that so much was like the day Paul died. But this time, Larry, Porsha, and I were driving in Larry's cop car out to the Bridge over Troubled Waters. Sally and Mrs. Gretzky had taken Lech back to Mrs. Gretzky's place to wait for us. There was another person with us, another cop. He was a guy who worked with Larry, a big blonde guy named Ed.

I had promised Larry I would show him how Paul worked it, how Paul killed himself. What if I was wrong? Wasn't it a crazy idea? I knew if my demonstration didn't work, Larry would be out of excuses. No matter what his heart said, he would do his job. He'd take me in.

As I had requested, Larry had brought a gun of the same shape and weight as Paul's. He had tied a four-foot string to it. The gun was loaded with blanks.

I had a bottle of Cynar. Porsha had agreed to help.

By the time we arrived at the forest preserve, it had been raining for hours. We got out of the car and walked along the stream. Just like the day of Paul's death, the stream was running high and fast. Maybe my luck had changed.

We walked to the bridge. I opened the bottle of Cynar and poured out half.

I turned to Larry. "May I have the gun?"

Larry handed the gun to me. The four feet of string dangled down. One end was tied to the gun, exactly the same as the gun found in the stream. I could see that Larry was puzzled but hopeful. Maybe he was beginning to figure it out himself.

I walked to the edge of the stream and looked into the murky rushing water. Then I took a deep breath. Grabbing the loose end of the string that dangled from the gun, I tied it around the neck of the bottle. Then, holding onto the gun, I tossed the bottle into the water. It sank.

I pulled the bottle out and dumped out some more Cynar. Now the bottle was about a quarter full. I tossed it in again. This time it floated.

I pulled on the string and reeled in the bottle.

"Okay, here goes," I said. "Larry, you walk Porsha downstream to the willow where we found the broken piece from a Cynar bottle. Show her the place and then come back here."

"What—" Larry began.

"Trust me," I said with a grin.

Larry didn't smile back. He and Porsha walked off down the path. Ed just stood there. I could see he thought I was completely off my rocker, and he was just putting up with this. I know Larry had told him that if I couldn't do what I promised—show how Paul shot himself and managed to get the gun downstream—they'd take me in.

When Larry came back, I said to Ed, "Now go stand where I did the day I saw Paul shot."

Ed walked back to the place where the little orange pennant left by the police still hung from the spindly bush. The rain was pouring down more heavily now. A sudden flash of lightning to the east and then a huge peal of thunder rolled across the sky. I shivered.

I walked out onto the bridge and gently laid the gun tied to the quarter-full bottle of Cynar on the floor of the bridge. "Ed," I called. "Can you see me?"

"Just barely!" Ed called out.

"Can you see the gun and bottle?" I yelled to him.

"No!" Ed shouted back.

"Okay," I said to Larry. "Watch this." I picked up the bottle and, holding onto the gun, I dropped the bottle over the railing of the bridge on the side away from Ed. The bottle swung over the stream, suspended by the string. Then I yelled to Ed, "Here goes!" I turned away from Ed, pointed the gun in the air and fired. Then I let go of the gun and dropped to the floor of the bridge.

The weight of the bottle, even one-quarter full, pulled

the gun. It slipped from my hand and was pulled over the railing. As it fell, it banged against the bridge. I heard it splash into the water.

Ed came running up. He looked at me and then at Larry. "Where's the gun? I didn't see you throw it over."

"I didn't," I said. "It went over, though. Right, Larry?"

Larry was staring at the bridge in amazement. Slowly, as if in a trance, he walked to where the weight of the bottle had pulled the gun over the railing and into the stream. He looked down. Of course, the current had floated the bottle downstream. It was long gone.

Larry pointed to two new nicks in the bridge. They looked almost identical to the previous ones I had noticed there. The gun had made them when it went over.

Ed nodded and photographed the nicks. I think he had figured it out by this time because he no longer looked irritated.

The three of us walked along the path to where Porsha sat. She had a huge smile on her face. "Our lucky day," she said. "That bottle came floating downstream, carried by the current. I thought it would just float on by, but then it hit that rock there." She pointed to a partly submerged rock in the middle of the stream just beyond the willow roots. "The bottle hit the rock and broke," Porsha said. "And look!"

We all looked where she was pointing. A broken piece of Cynar bottle was wedged into the willow root, looking almost exactly like the piece I had found—and in almost the same place.

Porsha said, "The bottle came just zooming along on top of the water. I saw the string dragging behind in the water, but I couldn't see the gun. But I could tell the bottle was dragging something, from the look of the string. I bet you'll find the gun just about where you found Paul's. Cause once the bottle broke, the gun would go right to the bottom."

Ed shook his head in amazement.

"Paul must have really hated you, to do this to you, Janet," Larry said.

I felt sad. I couldn't help but feel for Paul. Imagining him standing in the rain, his heart full of anger and revenge and the pain of having killed the woman he loved. Did he think, as he called out to me and then raised the gun to his head, that punishing me would make it better?

I said, "I think he figured I deserved it. He thought I kept him from the woman he loved."

Ed was shaking his head. "That guy had a hell of a devious mind. I wouldn't have believed this would work if I hadn't seen it with my own eyes. I'll get a forensic team out here. We'll repeat this and take pictures. But I gotta say, this is amazing."

*   *   *

Larry drove us all back. He dropped Ed off at the station and then drove to my place and parked. Porsha ran to her apartment to tell her mother. I went into Mrs. Gretzky's. Sally was there. I hugged and kissed them both and thanked them. I would never have figured out what happened alone. We had thought it through together. I saw their happiness when I told them how well everything had gone and that the police now believed my story. I felt a great sense of contentment.

Mrs. Gretzky gave me a big hug. "Ach, you are soaked! Go up and get some dry things on or you will catch a cold," she told me.

I called to Lech. Outside Mrs. Gretzky's apartment, Larry was waiting. He walked me up to my door. He had worn a rain slicker, so he wasn't as wet as me.

"Would you like to come in and have a coffee?" I asked him.

"Yes, I would like that," he said, smiling at me. His smile lit up his face.

We three went in, Lech, Larry, and me. Larry went to the kitchen to make the coffee, Lech headed for his favorite spot on the living room rug, and I hurried to my room to change. I was soaked through.

My hair was past worrying about so I just dried it with a towel. But I put on a pretty outfit and spent some time trying to get my eye makeup on right. When I came out, Larry had made coffee and was sitting in the living room. As soon as he saw me, he came toward me and took me in his arms.

"It's over, Janet," he whispered. "You're safe now. There's no one after you."

"So many enemies," I said. "I feel like I must have done something wrong that so many people wanted to get me."

"No, no, no," Larry murmured softly. He kissed my neck and my cheek and my hair. "You smell good."

I pulled away. I couldn't yet take it in. It was all over. All the fear I had felt for so many weeks. And yet— "I still feel as if I killed them, Nita and Paul," I said to Larry. "If I hadn't interfered, they'd be alive today."

I realized I was shivering. Larry saw it too. He pulled me toward him and we sat down together on the couch, his arm around me, me resting against his shoulder.

"It's really all over between you and Pat?" he asked me.

I thought of my friend Sally. Despite everything Baxter had done, I knew she still loved him. But I did not feel that way about Pat. "Pat was my husband and nothing can undo that," I said. "He'll always be close to me in a way, I guess. But I don't love him. I don't want him in my life anymore."

"Do you want me in your life, Janet?" Larry asked.

Now that I was free of my fear, I could let myself take in what Larry had done. He had believed in me when no other man had. He had let me take risks and not tried to take away from me the chance to be strong and beat my enemies on my own. He had trusted me to look after myself, and at the same time he was there when I needed him. Was ever a woman so lucky?

I threw my arms around him and hugged him with all my strength.

"Yes, I do," I said.

"If I said I loved you, what would you think?" Larry asked me tenderly. "With everything that's happened, maybe you hate the very sound of the word *love*?"

"Not when you say it," I said to him. "Because you've taught me what it is."

He drew my face down to his. "I think we've learned together," he said.